CROOKED RIVER

MP MURPHY

GASLIGHT BOOKS
PRINTED IN CHARLESTON, SOUTH CAROLINA
2014

This book is a work of fiction. Names, characters, places, and incidents are products of the author's imagination or are used fictitiously. Any resemblance to actual events or locales or persons, living or dead, is entirely coincidental.

ISBN-13: 978-0692279069
ISBN-10: 0692279067

First Gaslight Books mass market edition August 2014

Manufactured by Gaslight Books in the United States of America
Printed in Charleston, South Carolina

For information regarding special discounts on bulk purchases, please contact Gaslight Books

For Linley

CROOKED RIVER

Prologue

She awoke on a strange sofa and slowly tried to sit up among the haze of her mind. The world around her began to spin, and her stomach screamed from the movement. It was a vain attempt and pushing any further would most certainly make her sick. She put her head back down as she tried to recall any memory that might help her discover where she was. From the safety of the black leather sofa, Chelsea looked out through the floor to ceiling window onto the blue expanse of Lake Erie. The coffee table in front of her was shaped like a piano, and fit right in with a room filled with music paraphernalia. It was coming together for her now, and the haze began to lift from her head. How she wound up in Bratenahl at Ian Zeitlin's lake side home, was something Chelsea still had trouble remembering, but at least she knew where she was.

Ian Zeitlin, once the curator of the Rock 'n' Roll Hall of Fame, had passed away nearly a year ago. The former curator had left everything to his only son, Levi, who now ran the Cleveland social circuits spending his inheritance. At the private Brookfield Academy, Chelsea had been friends with Levi, and they still traveled together in the same crowd of over-privileged kids. *Some after party*, Chelsea, thought, as she stretched and made a futile attempt to sit up again. She needed to stop her head from spinning. After a few minutes of slow, deep breathing, she found the courage for another try. Overcoming the warnings of her stomach, Chelsea finally forced herself upright and attempted to stay there. After a moment, she noticed her shoes on the floor, and her wristlet across the room on the table beside the window. Invoking what little strength she had, she managed to get both of her feet into her pumps without causing any more disturbances to her stomach. Now it was time to stand up.

A few minutes of sitting perfectly still gave Chelsea the control she needed to stand. Making her way onto her feet, she wobbled for a few seconds in her designer shoes and gingerly hobbled around the piano table towards her wristlet. Her world was a mess, and she was absolutely still drunk, or high, or both. A momentary loss of balance left Chelsea leaning with her head along the large, lake view window. The August heat radiated through the glass from outside, and for a brief moment Chelsea thought that today was going to be spent recovering by the pool. She slowly reached for her wristlet and with her other hand, balanced herself in attempt to turn towards the door.

From where she was standing, she noticed another person passed out, face down behind the couch.

She smiled and was glad there was someone else too wasted to make it home last night. The man appeared to be lying in spilled red wine, and the thought made her giggle out loud. He was surely worse off than she was. Chelsea began the slow walk towards the door when she decided the man on the floor should probably be woken up. Getting close enough to give the man a nudge with her foot, Chelsea paused and then released a bloodcurdling scream that reverberated throughout the empty home. As she screamed, her eyes glared at the gaping bullet wound in the back of the man's head, and she knew that it was blood the man was lying in, not wine.

Sobriety slammed into Chelsea like a semi truck as her scream broke off, and she realized she was alone with a dead body. Her legs started working before she even told them to. They moved her quickly out of the front door and down to the empty driveway. Where was her car? Did she drive last night, or did she leave her convertible downtown? As she fumbled for her phone hurrying to call a cab, she stopped, suddenly reminded of her situation. She had woken up alone in someone else's house with a dead body. There was no way she would let a cab pick her up here. Her adrenaline perked up again as she panicked, grasping for options. Chelsea was confused and scared as she stared at the shaking hand that held her phone. There was only one thing she could think of to do. She ran.

Chapter 1

The winding road along the river was a joy as I downshifted my Austin Healy convertible around an oak and maple shaded bend. I was coming down Chagrin River Road and into the exclusive hamlet of Gates Mills on the east side of Cleveland. I was a mere twenty minutes outside of the city, but it felt like I had been transported to colonial New England. Small stone walls lined the road, barely large enough for two cars, and the Chagrin River followed along as I pulled into the center of the small village. The center of Gates Mills was a picturesque cluster of early 19th century buildings, all painted flat white and complimented with black shutters. A series of water powered mills graced the banks of the meandering river, and a covered bridge highlighted the Norman Rockwell setting. I pulled the car up to the stop sign in the center of town, turned left onto Old Mills Road and accelerated under the covered bridge.

The river followed me on my right side, but I was no longer paying attention to its shallow, rippling waters. My focus was on the thickly, wooded left side of the road where, on occasion, a mailbox would guard a gravel drive. Neighborhoods in Gates Mills were nonexistent. Instead, the village was a series of well-hidden estates guarded by deep woods and anonymity. I finally came upon the mailbox I was looking for about three miles past the bridge. I slowly steered my car onto the pebbled drive and took in the reality of how untouched the woods around me seemed to be.

The drive took me about a mile into the forest before I finally came to the gate. A pair of large, black iron doors, attached to a stone wall, swung open as I approached. It seemed as if they were expecting me. Passing through the gates, I noticed the length of the stone wall as it disappeared into the woods. A series of security cameras placed about every hundred yards on the wall's face, stood sentry over the grounds. The gravel had now been transformed into blacktop, and the woods suddenly became freshly manicured lawns. Dark wood fences lined the drive and separated the lawn by sections. The fenced in areas contained scattered clusters of bay horses playing in the grass, except for one area that housed a lone gray colt. The drive was canopied by rows of fully matured oaks, purposely planted to create a tunnel effect over the driveway leading up to the house. It was amazing someone had the time and money to construct such an illusion.

First, I saw a fountain containing a sculpture of a horse and a ship, an odd combination had I not known the owner. Then as the canopy of oaks opened up, I finally caught a glimpse of the Tudor style mansion. Medieval wooden doors guarded the entrance to the expansive estate. Three stories, with turrets stretching higher, filled my vision, and suddenly I was in another world far away from the Cleveland I knew.

No one came out through the doors to greet me, so I parked my car where I felt appropriate, right out front, and made my way to the stairs. I looked for the doorbell and could not seem to find the button anywhere. Faced with my only other option, I lifted my hand to knock. Looking forward to banging on the large wooden doors, and the sound that would echo throughout the house, I was disappointed when they opened slowly, revealing a middle-aged man in a polished suit.

The man gave me a questioning glance, and I felt like I might have been in the wrong place, as if that were possible. "Jack Francis," I said, "I'm here to see Captain Gilmore."

"Yes, I am fully aware of who you are Mr. Francis. I am Douglas, the Captain's assistant." *More like his butler*, I thought. "He has been expecting you. He is on the back porch if you wish to follow," Douglas continued, with a wave of his hand towards the inner sanctum of the home.

I took one step inside and was immediately in awe of the opulence that presented itself. A magnificent hall, complete with chandelier and grand staircase, spread out in front of me. On the walls, I noticed a collection of American landscape paintings that could have belonged in the Cleveland Museum of Art and I paused for a moment to stare.

"Mr. Francis, Captain Gilmore, is waiting and not very patiently I might add."

"Right, sorry." I moved on, but slowly.

Chapter 2

The porch overlooked a private lake, which sparkled like diamonds, and was outlined by pine trees. A small dock had a center console fishing boat and a two-person sailboat tied to it. I could have gone for a little afternoon fishing, cold beer, a nap, and, if the fishing gods so wished, a few largemouth bass. There was no chance of that. I had work to do, and I was sure Douglas would have a conniption if I broke away from him and headed towards the dock.

"Mr. Francis," my thoughts were interrupted by Douglas's voice. "May I introduce you to Captain James Gilmore?"

Captain Gilmore was an old man and looked so in his Amish rocking chair. His legs were covered with a blanket, and he was smoking an obnoxious cigar. He was frail and into his eighties, but there were still signs of what was once an athletic body. The man had been hard and powerful in his younger years. The hardness had left him, but the power stayed and maybe even grew.

"Please to meet you sir," I extended my hand and he ignored it.

"Sit, we have much to discuss and I am tired. Douglas, please grab us something to drink while we talk. I believe Mr. Francis here would like some bourbon, Pappy Van Winkle 20 year old, if we still have any left, and I would like a brandy."

"But sir......,"

The Captain cut him off, "No buts, I would like a brandy."

"Very well," and Douglas disappeared.

The Captain did not say a word to me while Douglas was gone. He just sat taking small puffs on his cigar as he stared out onto the lake. "Captain," I began to ask but was stopped with a finger from the old man. Finally, Douglas returned, and we were graced with our drinks. The Pappy Van Winkle was a treat, a bourbon that I could only afford to partake in on special occasions. The Captain did his homework on me, but I had also done mine on him.

"Thank you for the bourbon, Captain. I see you have done a little research on me."

"Yes quite, I would not have asked you here otherwise. You see if I am to employ someone I need to be able to trust or distrust them completely. Does that make sense to you Mr. Francis?"

Actually it did. The man was looking for predictability in his employees. Predictable people were easy to control.

"I did some homework on you too."

I was not coming into this blind either. A request to visit the man's home could only mean important business.

"I would like to hear what you have."

"Ok, where should I start?"

"Start from the beginning that seems to be a reasonable place," he smiled almost enthusiastically at what I had to say about him.

"You were born to a business mogul who made his money investing into Standard Oil with Rockefeller. He sold his stock in the oil company and then used the profits to start a shipping company. There was not a whole lot of risk in the maneuver, as your father had already lined up a contract with his old partner to ship Rockefeller's oil from the refineries here in Cleveland to the rest of the world. In fact, I believe it was your father who moved the family out of their Euclid Avenue mansion and built the home we are currently sitting in."

"So far so good," the Captain said. It appeared like he was enjoying the trip down memory lane.

"From what I could gather the old man never spoiled you. In fact, you seemed to work hard in school and went for higher education at Kenyon College. Afterwards, you left home for a stint in the Navy before returning to Cleveland. Back in your hometown you joined the crew of one of your father's freighters and traveled as a simple crew member unbeknownst to the others on the ship."

"Not entirely true. There was a lad who joined up with me whom I trusted with the knowledge of who I was."

"Very well," I was on a roll with my story and the interruption was a distraction. "You worked your way up through the ranks and ended up becoming captain of your own vessel after a while. Unfortunately, the promotion would not be for long as your father would soon pass away. Finally, you were recalled to take over the company and managed to guide it to even more prosperity, an impressive task considering the decline of the oil and steel industries in Cleveland."

The Captain looked impressed with himself as he took a long draw on his cigar. "We needed to branch out," he said. "The company was expanding even before the collapse of the local economy and we survived globally." Yes, he was proud. "Mr. Francis, thank you for the trip through my past, but what can you tell me about my more recent life?"

"Let's see, the company is still thriving. I believe it to be one of the largest privately held companies in the country. Your personal life has not been so smooth, if you don't mind my saying."

"Not at all."

"You have two daughters, who have been a handful in part because of the age gap. Your wife, who passed away giving birth to your second daughter, was quite younger than you and wanted kids, so now you have a pair of girls in their twenties. Madeline, the oldest is twenty-seven and Chelsea is twenty-three."

"Correct. I have been weak in raising them without a mother, and they have become a handful to an old man. I love them very much, and that gives me the energy to carry on, and yet their actions continue to drain it from me. Mr. Francis, the reason you are here is because I am running out of energy and time to deal with my daughters. It appears the younger one, Chelsea, has found her way into some trouble — trouble I wish to keep hidden from her and anyone else, if I am making myself clear."

"I understand sir. No unnecessary publicity for the family."

"Exactly."

"What is it that I am here to help you with Captain?"

"Blackmail, Mr. Francis. Blackmail."

Chapter 3

In navy blue pinstriped suit and gleaming well-polished shoes, Daniel Shaw, exited from his routine lunch at Morton's and walked up Ontario Street towards his newest prized possession. A quick turn down Huron Road and Shaw was standing in front of the beautiful new Rock 'n' Roll Casino and Hotel. Unlike most casinos, Shaw's structure was comprised of large windows that allowed views of the city skyline, the Cuyahoga River, and from the top floors of the building, one could glimpse the blue waters of Lake Erie. In reality, the floors with the lake view were Shaw's own private space, keeping the public from ever catching sight of the sweet water sea.

The sliding glass doors opened as he entered the lobby, and immediately he was flanked by a pair of security guards. He hated security, but on the casino floor they insisted on escorting him. What he could not grasp was why in his own casino he needed their company, and yet he just walked across town by himself. If it were up to him, he would just get rid of them all. He grew up fighting for everything he had and knew how to take care of himself. To Shaw the only benefit of the security detail was the show of power it offered while he was on the casino floor.

When he got to the private elevator and inserted his key card, the two security thugs turned and went back to their post, leaving Shaw as he entered. The elevator had only four stops: the casino floor, the basement garage where he had a private spot for his car, the security offices, and the top floor office and suite that he had designed to escape his wife and home in the suburbs. When the elevator doors opened they brought Shaw to a room surrounded by glass windows that gave him a view of almost every part of the city. Had he left through the doors on the opposite side of the elevator, he would have been led to his private apartment, but not today, there was work to do.

In the open office space, he had a large bar, Persian rugs covering hardwood floors, numerous flat screens to watch the action on the casino floor or the ball game, and his favorite possession, an antique desk he had discovered on a trip to Charleston, South Carolina. He plopped himself down on the leather chair behind the desk and picked up the phone.

"Jillian."

"Yes, Mr. Shaw."

"Get me Lee Kershaw on the phone."

"Yes Sir, just one moment."

She was not the brightest woman in the world, but Jillian made a great secretary. She had the looks to impress people who visited his office, most of which he had paid for, and she knew how to give a good blow job when needed. Her best asset, however, was that she did what she was told and never asked any questions. The last part was mandatory in the casino business.

"Lee Kershaw on the line," Jillian came back on the phone.

"Thank you Jillian. Lee, what do you have for me on that little project I gave you?"

"Well Mr. Shaw it's not quite done yet. We had a small slip up."

"We?"

"I sent Jimmy DeLuca out on this assignment and well, he kind of got a little sloppy."

"That little Italian putz. The two of you better fix it......whatever the hell it is you did."

"Well, what happen was," Lee Kershaw was stammering a little as he spoke.

"I don't give a crap about what happened. I paid you to do a job. Now finish it correctly or else we are going to have a problem. We both know that I don't like problems Lee, so fix this and fix it fast."

"Yes Mr. Shaw. I'll get back to you when," but it was too late to finish, Shaw had already slammed the phone down.

Chapter 4

The Clevelander Bar was packed with the after work crowd. Even with the air conditioning pumping through the vents and ancient fans turning from the cavernous ceilings, the place was still muggy. Kershaw walked through the bar still fuming from the phone call with Daniel Shaw. The man was an egotistical maniac, but he was powerful and he paid well. Kershaw knew he had screwed up by sending out Jimmy DeLuca and now he regretted it even more than he thought he ever would. The kid had been getting sloppy and overconfident lately, which was a bad combination in the business they were in. Eventually that combination would get you killed.

Kershaw scanned the bar and found the spot he was looking for. He saddle up next to a knockout of a brunette and ordered a beer. Soft curls of hair framed a perfect face and voluptuous lips that were sipping a gin and tonic. She wore tan suit pants and had a fitted white blouse tucked in. Kershaw followed the lines of her thighs up to her thin waist and to the spot where her blouse was unbuttoned giving him a glimpse of her ample cleavage.

"Quit staring at my tits Lee," the woman said not even giving him a glance.

"Sorry Alex, but they're just out there for public viewing."

"Go screw yourself asshole."

"Hey that was a compliment."

"I don't see how."

"Well that's what it was."

"Fine, what the hell are you doing here?"

"I have a job for you. More like a problem to fix." Kershaw didn't like the idea of passing along these jobs, but he did not have the manpower to fix this one. Alex was reliable and ruthless so she would not be a problem like Jimmy had been.

"I'm listening. Normal fee just so you know."

"If you get it done fast there will be a little extra for you."

"Hmm...you must be working for the big guy if you're throwing around extra cash."

"That doesn't matter Alex. Now listen I need you to find an antique dealer for me."

"You've got to be kidding? That should be easy."

"Not exactly, there is a good chance you will not be the only one looking for him, and I bet he knows it. The way I look at it, he'll be keeping a low profile unless the guy is a plain idiot."

"What's he done?"

"Gotten into affairs where he doesn't belong."

"You want to fill me in Lee?"

"Not here. Get in touch with Jimmy DeLuca. He's your muscle on this one and the one who got us into the mess. He will fill you in on all the details, but remember to keep a leash on the kid because he's gotten a little sloppy."

"Can you give me the antique dealer's name at least?"

"Charles Beard. He's got a shop over near the market on West 25th Street. Check the place out first. Probably won't find anything, but it will be a good place to start."

"What are we looking for?"

"Just look for Beard. Like I said before, Jimmy will be able to give you more details."

"Fine, fine, I get the picture."

"This is really important Alex. Get it done fast and get it done right. No screw ups this time or we might all be looking for a place to hide." Kershaw got up from the bar stool and threw some cash down for his beer. "No change," he said to the bartender who had come over.

"Thanks," the bartender picked up the cash and walked away.

"Lee, what kind of time frame do I have? I mean what does getting it done fast entail?"

"Yesterday Alex, does that paint the picture for you?"

"Sure does, now remind me to thank you for bringing me into this someday."

"You're just finding a simple antique dealer, remember?"

"I know you Lee, and it's always more complicated than you lead on."

Kershaw nodded to Alex and left her sitting at the bar. She would get the job done. He had no doubts or no choice in the matter.

Chapter 5

The pictures the Captain handed me were enough to make a man worry, but the blackmailer's note was what really had me puzzled. The pictures were simple and predictable, yet they were still a gruesome image portraying Chelsea standing above an unidentified man with a hole blown through the back of his skull. It was the note, though, that had me guessing. It was signed, which was completely unprofessional. Signed, I thought, it was actually signed. Who signed a blackmail note? Who would be dumb enough to actually put a bull's-eye on their back? Even the most confident crooks would not have been so dumb. The only answer was simply that the guy was an amateur, a complete fool who stumbled upon more than he could imagine.

"He signed it," I said in disbelief to the Captain.

"Charles Beard, antique dealer to Cleveland's elite. Runs a small shop over on West 25th near the market and across from the brewery, but he doesn't do a whole lot of business out of the store."

"Why not?"

"The man specializes in the rarest of pieces. His shop is not the place an average antique collector would go into to purchase a piece. No, Charles Beard is a finder. You tell him what you are looking for and he goes out and gets it, no matter what the cost. That is the reason he deals with only people who can afford such a service."

"I understand the business, but why would he blackmail your family?"

"Why do you think?" The Captain wanted my opinion of the situation. He must be testing my judgment I guessed.

"He's an amateur who stumbled on an opportunity. Beard probably was delivering a piece to this house," I pointed to the picture in my hand, "and walked in on the scene."

"It's the Zeitlin house over in Bratenahl," the Captain offered.

"How do you know?"

"Look at the background, all the extravagance and the wall memorabilia. I have been in that obnoxious house and wouldn't forget it."

"OK, so he was delivering a piece to the Zeitlin house and stumbled upon this scene. He recognized Chelsea because he has done business with you," I looked at the Captain for confirmation.

"Yes, we have done business and yes, he knows who Chelsea is."

"So he snapped a few shots with his camera phone, and figured he would extract his retirement from you."

"Apparently so."

"What do you want me to do with this guy?"

"Anything, I do not particularly care. All I want is to get back anything he has on Chelsea. Mr. Francis, my family means the world to me and I will do anything to protect them. I am not telling you to do anything outside of the law, but I want you to understand my need to protect my daughter."

"I believe I'm getting your point," I answered him confidently.

"Nothing comes back to this house. None of this will ever reach the ears of the public, and under no circumstances do I ever want my daughter to find out."

"You mean she doesn't know?"

"No, and she won't. Chelsea is not the most stable of creatures, never has been. I can't imagine how such a fragile girl would react to being blackmailed. I am sure she is already a complete mess over finding herself next to a dead body."

"Has she spoken of this at all to you? Does she know who the dead guy in the picture is?"

"She hasn't said a word and I am sure she won't. As for the body, who knows? It is not a priority of mine. You do understand what I want from you Mr. Francis?"

"Yeah, get any evidence that Beard has on Chelsea and neutralize this problem with no public knowledge."

"That's the military precision I expected out of you." The Captain closed his eyes and rested his head on the back of the rocking chair. I thought he had fallen asleep for a second.

"If that is all Captain?" I rose believing the conversation had ended with the man falling asleep.

He opened his eyes suddenly. "That is all. We will not speak on this subject again, you and I. If you need anything you will contact Douglas. He will also pay whatever fees you may accumulate." The man returned his head to the back of the chair and closed his eyes.

"I understand Captain, and thank you for the bourbon," I put the glass down next to the photos and made my way towards the door.

"Mr. Francis," the old man came alive again.

"Yes."

"My daughter is the only priority here. Do you understand?"

"I get the picture sir."

"Very well then, end this quickly."

Chapter 6

Madeline rose quickly from her chair on the upstairs balcony of her father's estate. She moved fast and quietly, with her long, tanned legs moving her into her room where she threw a robe on over her bikini. Opening the door, she proceeded down the hall on tiptoes. Madeline was determined to see who this Mr. Francis was. She had overheard her father's entire conversation with the man, and now she needed to know who was entrusted with Chelsea's well-being.

At the edge of the main hall and behind the central staircase, she began to hear the voices coming from below. She slowed, and positioned herself behind a marble pillar, conveniently putting herself in the shadows on the second floor. Below her in the main hall, she could see Douglas speaking with a man. Average height, maybe a little short for her taste, but he did have a nice body. *Athletic*, she thought, *that could make up for the height*. He had a firm jaw, dark hair, and piercing blue eyes. She found herself paying attention to the man's looks and not the conversation. She shook her head, clearing her mind, and concentrated on the conversation.

"I have been authorized to give you a check in the necessary amount right now Mr. Francis," Madeline heard Douglas say.

"A butler with the ability to write checks, I am impressed."

"I am Captain Gilmore's assistant, not his butler, Mr. Francis."

"Sorry, I misunderstood."

Madeline watched the man smile.

"Hold onto the check. I haven't done anything for the Captain yet, but I will be in touch."

"I will be waiting, sir."

"Douglas, just so you know I do charge for my expenses while on the case as well."

"The Captain has given me quite a large sum to provide to you now, and then more if he is satisfied with your work. Needless to say, I do not think your expenses will be a problem. I am to remind you that the sensitive nature of your work is a priceless commodity to him."

"I am beginning to understand that Douglas," Mr. Francis went for the door, "I'll be in touch."

"Good day, Mr. Francis."

Madeline watched the man walk out of the front door and waited until she heard his car pull away before she headed back to her room. There was opportunity here for her, but first she needed to protect Chelsea. Her father looked upon her often as a nuisance, similar to her little sister, but he didn't realize how much she kept Chelsea out of trouble. Madeline had her own problems, true, but now she needed to put them aside to take care of her sister. *This Mr. Francis was the key*, she thought. She would stay close to him until he could provide her with the information she needed to put an end to this episode on her own, and besides, from the looks of him, it was going to be good company.

Chapter 7

I replayed the situation over and over in my head the whole way back downtown from the Captain's house. There was a certain peculiarity to the entire state of things that I couldn't seem to put my finger on. Besides, now I had a feeling that it was going to get a little more complicated than the Captain had planned. I was pretty sure that someone was listening in on my conversation with Douglas. I could have sworn there was a woman in the shadows on the second floor balcony. If there was, I would bet that either one, or both, of the Captain's daughters now knew about the blackmailer.

Parking the car in the basement garage of my condo building in the Warehouse District, I quickly ran up to my place to change. It was a top floor condo I had been able to swindle, for mere pennies of what it had been worth before the housing market had crashed, and now I lived like a gypsy in the palace. There was nothing better than lake views by day and the lights of the city by night.

I tore off the suit I felt was necessary to wear for my meeting with the Captain, and replaced it with a pair of shorts and a polo. It was the middle of August after all. Looking at the clock in my bedroom I realized it was time for happy hour, so I made my way back down to the street and hailed a cab. I could have walked the short ten blocks from my condo on West 6th Street over to East 4th were I was headed, but I was feeling lazy and it was hot.

East 4th is a pedestrian only street filled with clubs, bars, and restaurants. It was also home to my favorite happy hour spot, the Greenhouse Tavern. I walked through the glass front door, into a building two stories tall. The place was narrow but long, and the bar ran down the right side. There was balcony seating on the second floor that overlooked the bar, and large windows that faced the street, but at the moment no one was eating. I was alone at the restaurant's oversized, beast of a bar. There were a few cooks speaking with the chef at a table, and Katya was in her usual place behind the bar.

Katya was about the purest of American sweethearts. She had big, brown, puppy dog eyes that matched her straight, shoulder length hair. The woman had the looks of a high school prom queen and a personality to boot. I should have scooped her up years ago but I was too late, as a diamond already sparkled on her finger. Before I even sat down she had a bourbon on the rocks already on the bar, and if I had to guess, a plate of gravy frites would be out for me any minute. It wasn't that I came here often, which I did, but Katya knew me well having married my former partner when I was in the FBI.

I was always too social in school, never paying much attention to my studies, so when I dropped out of college at Ohio State I joined the Army. It was the structure of the military that worked on me, and despite my carefree attitude about most things in life, I excelled. Eventually the Bureau noticed me and sent me to The Farm for training. Federal work is a stable career when you're not being shot at, but the problem is it didn't pay well. I stayed on for ten years, mostly because I was stationed in Cleveland and enjoyed working with my partner, Colin Sommers. When I finally had enough, I moved into the private sector where the money was better. I tried to take Colin with me but he wouldn't budge. I think it was the stability that kept him there, especially since he had just married Katya.

My gravy frites came within a few minutes, and I devoured the bowl of brown gravy and mozzarella curd covered fries before they even cooled off. Katya and I were having small talk while a few more people wandered in. I knew by six o'clock the whole street would be crawling with suits from every office building downtown. I was not here for the crowd and I actually didn't come here to eat and drink, although that part always helped. I was waiting for my old partner to get off work. He always stopped in and I needed to run my day by him. The Captain wanted to keep the whole affair quiet, but I needed an outside opinion of what I was getting myself into. Colin always had a clearer head than I did.

Chapter 8

"I see you're here hitting on my wife again," Colin said as he entered the bar. He threw his jacket over the barstool and loosened his tie. His boxy frame stretched out his button-down shirt and his blonde hair seemed a little too stiff today.

"And I see you're going a little heavy on the mousse again."

Katya giggled. "I keep telling him to go a little more natural with the hair, but he refuses. Must be a Bureau thing."

"Not when I was there."

"Shut up, both of you," Colin said sitting down next to me. Katya walked away to take care of some other guests leaving her husband with a cold beer. "So what's up with you? Did you spend all afternoon in the bar?"

"Nah, I just got here. I was looking for you, actually."

"Why is that?"

"Had an interesting day."

"You want to run it by me?" Colin asked, sipping his beer.

"I had to run out to Gates Mills today to meet with a client."

"Captain Gilmore?"

"How did you know?" Now I was a little thrown off.

"I recommended you when he called looking for help."

"Why would he call you? From what I gathered he didn't want word about this whole thing getting out?"

"He called me because he knew I could keep it a private matter. It was a personal call not a Bureau call."

"Still doesn't explain why he called you."

Colin pointed with his beer toward Katya. "I'm married to his goddaughter."

"Now, how come I never knew about this?"

"I don't know how you didn't. The Captain and you were both at our wedding."

"I don't really remember."

"I'm not surprised," Colin chuckled.

"What did he tell you about this whole thing?" I was curious to know just how involved Colin already was.

"Everything I guess. At least I'm sure it was the same thing he told you."

"Have you seen the pictures of Chelsea?"

"No we just talked over the phone. I don't think he would show me anyways because to him I'm still the authorities."

"Did it seem strange to you how unconcerned he was about the dead body? When we talked he just skimmed by it and kept focusing on Chelsea."

"The man is steadfast in protecting those girls, even if they give him trouble. The Captain was a ruthless business man and never had any pity for anyone else. I'm sure it was the same with the body in the picture. He didn't care because it didn't concern him."

"Could be," I thought for a minute. The body was still bugging me. "Did you guys ever get an I.D. on the corpse?"

"Now there's a funny thing. There hasn't been a corpse reported, and it gets worse."

"How's that?"

"I'm not officially involved so I couldn't send anyone over to the Zeitlin place to check it out, but I did go over on my own."

"And?"

"And the place was clean, empty, no body."

I was stunned. "How can that be?"

"Looked like a professional job to me. Oh, I'm sure if I had sent some of the techies over there they could have dug something up, but once again I'm not officially on the case."

"Simple blackmailing job with a first time crook was how the Captain laid it out to me. I think it just became a little more than that."

"You want my advice?" Colin asked, face smug, and arms crossed at his chest. "Stay out of it. Find the antique dealer and get back anything he has on Chelsea. Then collect your money from the Captain and forget about it. Just stay out of whatever else comes along."

"We both know I can never just let things be. It's not in my nature. The whole thing will just eat at me and I will have to keep digging to satisfy my own curiosity"

"I know. That is why I recommended you to the Captain." Colin was beaming now. "But don't forget what curiosity did to the cat."

Chapter 9

It was lunchtime and the street was bustling with people running to and from work on their short breaks. The wind had begun to kick up out of the northeast blowing in between buildings and rustling the trees. A storm was coming. Madeline sat, parked in her silver Mercedes, watching the storefront of Charles Beard's antique shop and all was quiet. It had been quiet all morning. No movement in or out and no sign of Beard himself. She should have known the slimy bastard would keep a low profile, but then some people didn't know any better.

The hours of sitting patiently were wearing on her and she was getting anxious. Mr. Francis wasn't at his condo when she drove there earlier, and she figured he would at least stop by Beard's shop today. Instead, she had seen nothing. Madeline reached for her keys and was getting ready to turn on the ignition, when her cell phone vibrated in the seat next to her. It was Chelsea. She had a feeling that she would regret telling the poor girl about the predicament she was in, but she had a right to know.

"What is it Chelsea?" Madeline answered.

"Maddie, where are you? What's going on?" The girl sounded like she was panting as she rattled off questions.

"Slow down. Nothing has happened yet. I'm just sitting outside of Beard's shop waiting for someone to show up."

"You're just sitting there? All morning you've just been sitting there. We need to do something."

"Chelsea, you need to relax and have some patience. We cannot just run into this thing head first. If we make any mistakes it will make things worse, so just relax."

"I can't relax. I'm trapped in this damn house pacing around my bedroom like a crazy person. I feel helpless in here. Please give me something, anything to make me feel better, please!" Chelsea sounded desperate and Madeline knew that was not a good thing. The drugs had made her more unstable than she normally was, and now without them, without being able to go out, and being stuck in that house with their father, Madeline knew it was a dangerous combination.

"I understand Chelsea, I really do. Just please give me some more time."

"I need something. I need to do something. I can't just sit here anymore. Please give me something I can use. Give me something, something good. I just want the whole thing finished. I'm nervous, scared, and what if someone comes for me. They killed that poor man. His head was ripped open and blood was all over the floor. I was right there and I saw it. They could come and do the same thing to me." Chelsea had not been able to get rid of the nightmare. She had no idea who the dead man was, said she was too scared to look at his face. She also had not been able to grasp the fact that if they wanted her dead they could have shot her that night. A tangled web of fear and anxiety was creating a different reality for the girl.

"Chelsea just give me a few more hours and I'll get you something I promise." Madeline looked up towards Beard's shop in time to see two people, a brunette woman and a young Italian-looking man peeking into the front window of the store. They spoke to each other for a moment and the man disappeared down an alley around the back of the building. The brunette woman, attractive in her pressed suit, waited calmly out front until the door opened from the inside. "Chelsea, something's going on I got to go."

"Maddie! Maddie, what is it? Maddie!" Madeline heard none of her sister's pleas. She had already hung up the phone intently watching the store. A couple of blocks down the street, making their way towards the shop, walked two men. Madeline noticed them just as they came up to Beard's antique store. "Oh, Shit," she said out loud. It was going to get interesting. Mr. Francis was walking in the front door of the shop with none other than Agent Colin Sommers. A lot of people were looking for Charles Beard today.

Chapter 10

The girl was losing it, Douglas thought, as he walked down the hall and away from Chelsea's room. He had overheard her phone call with Madeline leading him to the conclusion that both girls were aware of the blackmailer. It only made sense and would explain the way Chelsea had been acting lately. Just now he had left the girl, talking frantically to herself alone in the room. Sure, drug abuse played a part and she was not the most stable of people to begin with, but now Douglas would say she was near the edge of reality. Frantic, unpredictable, and drugged up past any reasonable point, was a combination not to be allowed to fester without some type of supervision.

The front study of the Gilmore mansion had the look of a library. An eighteen-foot ceiling towered overhead with extensive molding work and a conservative chandelier in the center. Four walls were adorned with bookshelves containing volumes collected by Captain Gilmore and his father. The ornate, mahogany desk was surrounded by a fireplace, large, plush leather sofas, and windows that overlooked the drive and the grazing horses. The desk was bare except for a small lamp, Douglas's laptop, and a telephone. Douglas had found over the years that the study was the best place to conduct his business. The old man rarely entered the place and the girls probably had no clue that the room existed at all. Douglas had never seen either of them reading anything heavier than the weekly gossip column.

Retrieving a phone number off of his laptop, Douglas dialed the phone at the desk. Chelsea needed to be looked after closely and he had just the person to do it.

"Yes," a raspy, quiet voice answered.

"It's Douglas."

"I am aware of who it is," slight accent, maybe East European.

"There is something I need you to do."

"So soon? It seems like I just finished up the last job you sent me on. I am not accustomed to hearing from you so often."

"Yes, well, this is important," the man always made Douglas a little nervous and his voice quivered.

"What may I help you with then?"

"I need you to follow Chelsea."

A soft chuckle came from the other end of the line. "When Captain Gilmore gave you my number it was to handle important business affairs for him, and that is all."

"But this is important. The girl is out of control."

"I am not a babysitter," the raspy voice rose, not yelling, just pronouncing his disdain for the idea, "besides the girl has always been out of control."

"She could create problems for some of the Captain's businesses if she is left to her own devices. The girls, both of them, have found out about the blackmailer. It appears Madeline is trying to take care of it on her own, while Chelsea has increasingly drifted towards crazy. Her mind is too weak to handle such news. I am afraid that she will break and do something that we will be forced to clean up."

"I see," the voice paused for a second and Douglas thought he had hung up the phone. "Does Captain Gilmore know about this?"

"No he has washed his hands of the matter and left me to clean it up."

"And now you want me to clean it up for you?"

"No, I want you to prevent any further incidents by following Chelsea and keeping her from creating anymore problems for the Captain."

"Double what you paid me last time." This was not a question but a demand.

"Done, I'll transfer the money as soon as we are off the phone."

"Very well then." The voice was gone and the line when dead.

Douglas felt better just by getting off the phone with that man. He had no idea who he was, but all the same, any task he was given was completed perfectly. Still, his voice sent chills through Douglas's body. The man was a cold player, ruthless and effective, even though many of his techniques were quite abstract and gruesome.

There were feet scrambling down the front stairs and a loud slamming of the large door that led to the driveway. Within seconds, Douglas heard a car start and then from the window he caught a glimpse of Chelsea driving off in the car her father had given her for her sixteenth birthday. The car had sat in the garage for years, but Chelsea had been driving it the past few days. Douglas found that odd, but he assumed the girl had lost her other car while on one of her drinking binges. Unfortunately, those were the kinds of things one had to get use to when dealing with Chelsea. The missing car didn't bother Douglas nearly as much as her leaving the house, and in such a maddening way. Hopefully her new handler could find her before she did anything dramatic, but then again dramatic was Chelsea's nature.

Chapter 11

The girl behind the desk could have belonged there, but for a brief moment, her startled look at my arrival with Colin, gave her away. She recovered quickly, however, and adjusted her well-trimmed suit as she came out from behind the desk to greet us. Her brown hair bounced as she walked and so did other things on her. Each stride was confident as she reached out her hand to introduce herself.

"Hi, my name is Alex, Mr. Beard's assistant. What can I help you with today?" Her smile was big, white, and for a moment I thought I saw a sparkle.

"We'd like to speak with Mr. Beard if we could," I asked. Colin stayed quiet and walked around the barren store. The shop was sparse, and did not fit the image I had of an antique store. My memory of an antique store was a barn stocked full of odd pieces, so cluttered you could barely walk around. Every other antique shop in Ohio looked like that, but Charles Beard's store was different.

"I'm sorry, Mr. Beard is unavailable today. Can I maybe assist you in something?"

"No, it's important that we speak with him ourselves." There was noise coming from the back room and Colin began to stride over to the door. "Is he in then?" I gestured in that direction.

"No, no," Alex quickly cut off Colin's path to the door. "No, he's not in. That's just a stock boy we have moving a few things for us." She got Colin to move back around in front of the desk and then situated herself on top of it. "Like I said, is there anything I could help you two gentlemen with today?"

"And like I said, we need to speak to Mr. Beard personally. He would find it most beneficial to talk with us at the quickest and most opportune time."

"A private matter then, very well do you have a card I could pass along to Mr. Beard?"

I reached in my pocket for a card. Took out a pen and wrote something on the back of it. Colin looked at me questioning my actions. "Alex," I asked, "Do you have a boyfriend?"

"No."

"Ah, married then?"

"No. What is this about?" I had thrown her off guard.

I handed Alex my card. "My business number is on the front. That is for Mr. Beard. On the back I put my personal cell number and that is for you. I understand if you don't want to, but I would love to have drinks some time."

Alex smiled politely. "I will pass this along to Mr. Beard."

"Thank you." Colin and I turned for the front door knowing we weren't going to get any further with the woman. "Have a good day Alex."

"Good day to you Mr. Francis," she said looking at my card.

Once the door closed behind us, Colin turned to me as we walked across the street towards Great Lakes Brewery. "What the hell was that about? Is every girl you meet a possible date to you?"

"Yes, but I had good reason."

"What's that?"

"Well, we both know that Charles Beard works alone, no assistant and especially no stock boy, so she was there tossing the place."

"And so you asked out a potential criminal."

"I figure whoever she is working for will be just as curious about us as we are about her. I mean come on Colin, she knows we weren't there for antiques. You practically scream Federal Agent. I figured asking her out might move things along a little faster, you know, get to know her a little bit and feel her out."

"Whatever," Colin said. "You might want to watch yourself though. You end up pissing off most of the women you date, and this one is liable to kill you in your sleep or while you're feeling her out."

"Come on, it will be fine. What do I have to do to make you feel better about this?"

"Buy me a beer," he said heading through the front door of the brewery's pub.

Chapter 12

Some say Eliot Ness, when he had lived and worked in Cleveland, visited the Great Lakes Brewery pub often. These same people point to the bullet holes in the large wooden bar and will tell you they were made by Ness's gun. Whether the story is true or not I like to believe it. Every time I enter the place I am transported back to the age of mobsters, prohibition, and to an era I pictured as being more romantic than it actually was. I swear even today the bar at Great Lakes Brewery has a classic 1930s aura to it.

Colin and I sat at the end of the bar close to the door. There were two empty seats to my left and Colin had about a half dozen to his right. We could stake out Beard's shop from where we sat just by looking out the window. Jerry, the bartender, put two Dortmunders in front of us to help with the stake out. He was fifty-something and balding, but had enough sense of it to shave his head. Round, thin frames sat on his nose and made his eyes seem buggy. His cracked lips did nothing to help his already dismal appearance. Jerry's gift was by no means his looks. It was his longevity behind the bar that we were after. When you have been around as long as he had, you knew everything that was going on in the neighborhood.

"Jack just gave his number to Charles Beard's new assistant. Think he's got a chance?" Colin was talking to Jerry and I was pretending not to listen.

"That's strange I didn't know Mr. Beard hired an assistant."

"What about a stock boy?" Colin asked.

"I doubt it, the man's worked alone the whole time he's been across the street there."

"Boy, Jerry you're losing your touch. Back in the day you didn't miss a thing."

"A lot of strange things are going on there lately. In fact Mr. Beard seems to be ill or something." Jerry's voice was surprisingly strong and confident, which was a contrast to his drab looks.

"Sick? Why do you say that?"

"Haven't seen the man in a few days. Mr. Beard used to be as predictable as the Indians losing the Central Division. Every day at five he would stop in and have one beer, just one, and then walk home for the night."

"Any idea how many days it's been?" Colin was still asking the questions and I was still pretending to not pay attention. Sometimes it was just better to let Colin do the work.

"Oh, let me see, this is probably the third afternoon that I haven't seen him. Usually I see him walking to work in the morning when I am opening up and then again at lunch. He usually walks over to the market when it's open. On days it's not he eats at the Middle Eastern place around the corner."

"No sign of him at all?"

"Nope. Now how about you tell me about this assistant you say he's taken on."

"Well," Colin started, "we just left Beard's shop and she was there."

"She's there now?" Jerry appeared puzzled.

"Sure is, greeted us when we walked in. An attractive thing to say the least."

"That seems a little funny. Beard hiring an assistant that is."

"Jerry, we thought the same thing."

I had been caught up in Colin and Jerry's conversation and I forgot to watch the window. A woman had walked into the bar without me noticing. She had a strong, lean figure with strawberry blonde hair tied up in a ponytail that swayed as she moved. Her white, three-quarter length sleeve blouse, with a high, crisp, collar, left no doubt that her breasts moved in rhythm with her ponytail. The woman's long legs were accented by a tight khaki skirt and high heels. I personally enjoyed the light freckles that dotted her nose and stretched out across her cheek bones.

"Sonofabitch!" was all Colin could get out before she was in range.

"Colin, how are you?" The woman asked. "Jerry, may I have a Maker's on the rocks please. And you must be Mr. Francis?" She didn't even ask to sit down next to me, just threw her purse on the bar top and slid in beside me.

My first thought was that it was my lucky day, but one look from Colin told me otherwise. She did look familiar and I tried to place the face. My mind had been too focused on the incident in Beard's shop to have any chance at coming to a conclusion in the seconds I had.

"Jack," Colin said, "let me introduce you to Madeline Gilmore."

It clicked and my face must have been priceless because the woman giggled. "My pleasure," was all I got out as I extended a hand.

"You look surprised Mr. Francis."

"Please, it's just Jack."

"I'm sorry Jack, it's just I heard my father calling you Mr. Francis so I guess it's programmed in."

If I showed surprise before I would have hated to see my face now. Madeline's appearance was definitely not a coincidence.

Chapter 13

Jimmy stuck his head out from the back room of Charles Beard's shop. "What was that about?"

"I'm not sure. Have you found anything back there yet?"

"Alex, do you really believe that Beard was dumb enough to leave it stashed here?"

"No I don't. Slimeball's probably got it on him."

"Then why are we still here?"

"Jimmy, we are being careful now because you weren't before. If you tried to be more thorough in your work then we wouldn't be here at all, understand?"

"Yeah whatever, I messed up. Now get off my back. Who were those two guys anyways?"

Alex still held Jack Francis's business card in her hand twirling it between her fingers as she sat on Beard's desk. "Not sure."

"Cops?"

"No, I don't think so."

"Hired thugs then?"

"No Jimmy, you're already here."

"Well they sure as hell weren't antique collectors, so what then?"

"They weren't cops but they felt like it. Still, I'm pretty sure they weren't. The one that never said a word felt like a Fed, but not this Jack Francis." She held the business card for Jimmy to see.

"Oh yeah, what was he then?"

"Something more, he was a little too debonair to be with the Feds, but he could be in the private sector."

"Maybe the boss man hired them too."

"I doubt it Jimmy."

"But maybe," Jimmy got excited trying to figure out who the men where.

"Yeah maybe, but we need to know more."

Alex could hear Jimmy rummaging for something and then stopped. "There ain't nothing here. Let's go over to Beard's house and tear it apart. If he's there we can make him squirm a little bit too."

"Not so fast. Remember we are being careful. Sometimes I feel like I am babysitting you."

"Shut it Alex."

Ignoring Jimmy's bark and his threatening face, Alex continued talking mostly to herself. "I need to do some research on Jack Francis and his partner before we move too quickly." Alex flipped the card over looking at the cell phone number handwritten on the back.

"Research huh?" Jimmy questioned, looking over her shoulder at the number.

"Go home, but keep yourself available. I still might need you tonight."

"To go see Mr. Beard?" Jimmy got excited at the thought of confronting the man.

"Maybe, but don't move unless I call you, and stay sober."

"Fine, I'll be at my apartment." Jimmy stormed off through the back. Alex really did feel like she was babysitting him sometimes.

Chapter 14

Madeline had seen the brunette leave Charles Beard's shop and got out of her car to follow her, but her instincts told her differently. Suddenly she found herself walking into the bar, sitting down next to Jack and Colin. It wasn't something she had thought through, just something that happened. She still wondered where the brunette was headed, but everyone always told her to follow your instincts and you would find what you need, even if it wasn't what you wanted.

"Interesting to see you here Madeline," Colin said. "I didn't realize that this was one of your normal haunts."

"I don't get on this side of town very often, but I saw the two of you walk in so I figured I would say hi."

"Just happened to be in the neighborhood?"

"Something like that."

"I thought maybe you had been sitting outside in your car watching over Beard's store," Jack interjected into the conversation. His tone was obviously not in the mood for games.

"Now that just sounds boring. I was in the neighborhood shopping in a few of the boutiques." Madeline lit up a sly and seductive smile that would make anyone believe what she was saying.

"Cut the crap. We both know you overheard your father and me talking the other day. Not to mention that before I left your house I actually saw you eavesdropping on me and Douglas."

"You're very observant Jack. What is it you do for a living?"

"I collect bottle blondes."

"That's too bad mine is natural," Madeline said tossing her ponytail.

"And not quite blonde."

"Like I said, you're a very observant man Jack, but with some time and a little training I'm sure I could get you past my hair."

"With you, it's not the hair that turns me off."

"Aren't we feisty today?"

"I just don't like being played. It's a turn off."

"Alright, will you two cut it out?" Colin interrupted Jack and Madeline's little game. "You both are annoying the piss out of me. I could cut the sexual tension in here with a knife."

"Fine," Madeline said. She had decided it was time to start playing it straight anyhow. These two had information she wanted and it would be a shame if they cut her off from it. "Well if we're all going to be straight with each other, why don't one of you fill me in on the brunette and the Italian-for-hire across the street at Beard's."

"What Italian?" Jack began to say when it dawned on him. "That must have been the noise coming from the back of the store. The stock boy Alex called him."

"Alex? Is that the woman?" Madeline asked.

"Yeah," Jack answered. He was about to explain what happened in the store when his phone vibrated across the bar top. The caller ID read private.

Chapter 15

"Jack Francis here," I answered my phone after waiting a few seconds, watching it vibrate its way across the bar.

"Mr. Francis, its Alex from Charles Beard's office. I hope you haven't forgotten me already."

I was a little caught off guard but I recovered well. "No, not at all. Did Mr. Beard receive my message yet?"

"No he hasn't been in yet."

"Well then," I was amused with our little game. Funny considering I nearly bit off Madeline's head for doing the same thing. Maybe one woman playing games was all I could handle, and Madeline shouldn't be playing games when I was trying to help her sister. "What can I do for you Alex?"

"Is your offer still available?"

"What offer might that be?"

"I'm pretty sure you offered to take me out for drinks tonight."

"I'm not sure I said that, Alex."

"It was something like that." She was playing cute using a flirtatious voice with a small hint of a giggle. I was shocked she had it in her.

"Well if that's the case I couldn't say no."

"Great, I can't wait. I'll meet you at the Clevelander around 7:00."

"I'll be there." The phone clicked off and I slipped the cell into my pocket.

"What was that about?" Colin asked.

"I'm meeting someone for drinks at 7:00."

"You're joking?"

"Nope," I smiled at him. A big grin that screamed, *How do you like me now?*

"How do these things manage to happen to you?"

"Lucky I guess," still grinning from ear to ear.

"She's going to kill you in your sleep you know."

"Come on Colin don't be so harsh. She's probably a really sweet girl."

"Who are you two talking about?" Madeline finally had enough and wanted to be part of the conversation.

"Alex," I answered. My smile disappeared and turned into a look that said, "Who else?"

"The woman from Beard's shop," Colin added.

"You have got to be kidding," Madeline seemed actually appalled at the idea.

"It's for research. I've got to find out who she is and who she's working for."

"Jack," Madeline said. "Do you really believe that she'll just spill her guts to you?"

"Believe it or not he has his ways," Colin said rolling his eyes. I just chuckled into my beer.

"Well then, Jack Francis," Madeline got up from her stool, "I believe I underestimated you."

"Where are you going? I thought we were going to exchange information." I still found all this amusing, but apparently I was the only one because Madeline was headed for the door.

"We will, but I have decided to hold off until you have finished your research. I would not want to be given only half of the story and I'm sure you'll do your best to probe her for information." Sarcasm coated her voice. "By the way, thanks for the drink." Madeline said goodbye to us with a seductive smile and a toss of her ponytail, and she marched out of the bar and down the street.

"So now I'm buying for both of you?"

"Looks like it," Colin said as he ordered another beer.

Chapter 16

When Alex approached the man at the bar she found him of extraordinary good looks. He was a little short though. Really just a man of average height, but Alex usually went for the tall ones. Still, his body seemed firm and athletic-looking and that was a plus. Alex smiled to herself as she sat down on the bar stool next to Jack Francis.

The Clevelander had emptied out considerably since the after work crowd had packed the place, and with it the heat and noise diminished as well. The space around them was nice and Alex appreciated the room to play her game. It was a game after all. Life usually was but some had higher risks than others. The game with Jack Francis had yet to reveal just how risky it might be.

"Hello Mr. Francis," Alex said as the bartender placed a gin and tonic in front of her.

"Please, just Jack. Come here often do you?" noticing the bartender's delivery of the unordered drink.

"Why Jack, are you insinuating that I spend too much time in bars?"

"Not at all, just this one."

They both had a small chuckle at the exchange and found it a convenient way to break the ice. There was a little air of awkwardness about the encounter. Not the type one would find at a first date. On second thought, maybe a little, but mixed in with the atmosphere of two fighters trying to figure out their attack.

"I am in here quite a bit," Alex said. "Good place to relax after a hard day."

"Antique business rough?" Jack asked, playing along with her ruse.

"Something like that. So tell me, what do you do Jack? Your business card explains very little."

"To be honest I'm not exactly sure what you might call it. An independent consultant maybe the best answer, but still that's a stretch."

"What about private investigator?"

Nice jab, Jack thought. "Sometimes I am but not usually. I usually prefer work in security consultations for private firms, but then if the price is right, I'll take anything."

Alex knew that most of the information Jack was telling her was worthless. Every bit of it she had already found before she arrived. In fact, it only took one phone call. Nevertheless, he seemed inclined to talk and that was a good thing. "Can I ask you something and get a straight answer Jack?"

"Only if I can do the same?"

"Deal, but behave yourself." Alex smiled at the man with her pouty lips. It was a great distraction of hers. "When you came to Charles Beard's shop today were you working a case?"

"Let me just say that I don't have a clue when it comes to antiques."

"And the guy you were with?"

"You said only one question Alex, remember?"

"Alright then it's your turn."

"Charles Beard does not have an assistant or anyone else working for him, so what were you doing at his shop today?"

Alex delayed her response with a sip of her drink. "Since we are being so honest with each other, I can honestly say I was there working."

"Except not for Charles Beard."

"Something like that," Alex said shrugging her shoulders.

"Wow, this conversation is just opening up a whole new world for me."

"Easy on the sarcasm, Jack. If you walked in here thinking it was going to be easy then you have me mistaken. I can tell you right now that I'm not that kind of girl. Try working at it a little bit, Jack, and you just might get what you want."

"Are we still talking about the same thing?"

"I hope so," she said with that seductive smile. "Now, how about you take me to dinner? A girl needs to eat after all."

"I can live with that and I think I know just the place."

The two got up and Jack threw cash on the bar for the drinks. Alex went out and hailed a cab for the two of them. As the cab pulled away from the curb, a silver Mercedes pulled onto the street behind it and followed a couple of cars back.

Chapter 17

Her naked form was highlighted by the moonlight that came in through the parted curtains. The shadows accented Alex's swaying hips as she sauntered over to the chair in the corner of my bedroom and began to dress. Soft brown curls kissed her bare shoulders and reminded me of the perfect form found on Greek sculptures. I laid there, mesmerized by her nakedness. A pair of dress slacks being pulled up her legs finally broke my stare.

The woman was trouble, I knew that, but somehow I still ended up in bed with her. I was a sucker and I knew that too. After dinner we had danced lightly around the topic of her life leaving out anything important. When we came back to my place for an after dinner drink I should have seen it for what it was: a distraction. I tried to press hard on a couple of questions, but her response was sex, great sex.

"It's not even midnight yet," I pleaded from the bed. "I am always game for another round."

"That's sweet, but I need to be going." She was still dressing unfortunately.

"I'm not asking you to stay over, just stay longer."

"You're such the romantic Jack."

"Thanks, but that was nothing more than a pathetic plea for more attention."

"I'm pretty sure you've had enough. I would hate to leave you over stimulated." She stood over me in nothing more than pants and high heels, naked on the top. Alex looked at me for a moment then smiling she turned back to reach for her shirt. "This is going to end badly."

"For one of us?"

"For both of us." The shirt was on now. She was leaving for sure. "We haven't been open with each other tonight, but I think we're smart enough to know that Charles Beard has something we're both after."

"And what might that be?"

"Shut it, Jack. My point is we could be working for the same person but I doubt it. So the only reasonable thing is to assume we are working against each other. That will leave one of us unable to complete the job, maybe both. Either way, it won't end well."

"Say you'll give it all up for me and then we can go back to bed," I joked.

"Jack, what I am trying to say is that no matter how much I enjoyed you in bed, if you get between me and what I am after I will run you through." The purse was over her shoulder and she was moving to the door.

"Where are you going Alex?"

"I'm going home to catch up on some work." A wicked smile crossed her face. "I'll see you later Jack. Get some sleep." She left shutting my bedroom door. I waited for a moment until I heard my front door shut before leaping out of bed and grabbing the clothes that had been tossed to the floor earlier.

Dressed, I raced out of my door to the elevator slamming my finger on the button impatiently. When the doors finally opened, the seconds it took to ride down to the street level seem like hours. An electronic bell sounded my arrival in the lobby of my condo building and I raced from the elevator and out onto the sidewalk. I was just in time to watch a cab turn the corner. Before I even had a chance to figure out my next move, a silver Mercedes came speeding up on the empty street. Pulling up to the curb with a screech, the passenger's side door swung open and a woman's voice said, "Get in." I paused.

The voice repeated. "Get in," this time with more authority, "quickly."

Chapter 18

The tires squealed on the black top as the eight-cylinder accelerated down my street and turned the corner to follow the cab. "A subtle exit," I said looking over at Madeline.

"Sorry the tires are a little low."

"Sure they are. You know, when you are following someone the idea is to not attract attention to yourself."

"Really funny guy, I've been following you all night and you didn't seem to notice."

"You've got a point. Wait, you've been following me? Why?"

"Why does anyone follow anybody?" Madeline smiled. I was left by one beautiful woman and fell into a car with another. What a lucky night. "I was looking for information that might help Chelsea. You figured to be my best lead and now it seems to be working out."

"She could just be heading home." I said to her.

"I doubt it."

"So do I."

We traveled in silence for a few minutes crossing the Detroit–Superior Bridge and turned into the Ohio City neighborhood. Large, maple trees lined the narrow streets that were home to old Victorian homes. Many of the houses were being refurbished, while others were still dilapidated and in need of love. We were mere blocks from Charles Beard's antique shop.

"Where is she going?" Madeline asked.

"I've got a good idea, Beard's house. He lives in this neighborhood somewhere."

"You haven't gone to see him there yet?"

"Nope, it didn't seem that urgent."

"How do you figure?"

"Well looking at it now, I guess it was pretty stupid not to have gone there yet, but I didn't think he was going anywhere since he was trying to get money out of your father."

"It would have been the first place I checked!" Madeline appeared annoyed with my investigation and she probably had reason.

"I was going to go first thing in the morning. In all honesty I figured he had run off to hide somewhere. I bet he is still in town, but why would he sit like a target in his house? I'm sure it will turn out to be another dead end like his shop." Madeline slowed the car as we turned a corner. I noticed the cab pulled over halfway down the street. "That must be it," I said as Madeline pulled her car behind a minivan to hide it.

"Has she gotten out yet? I can't really see."

"No she's just sitting there. Must be paying the cabby."

"Why would she come here this late and use a cab no less?"

"Got me, this whole thing seems strange. It sure doesn't seem like she's trying to be very secretive. It could be she just came by on a hunch." It was then that I noticed Alex getting out of the cab. A northeast wind had kicked up off of the lake earlier in the night and now it blew Alex's hair across her face. She paused to bend over, sticking her head into the cab window, and spoke to the driver. A moment later she straightened herself, brushing the hair from her face and headed toward the house. The cab stayed parked out front with the engine still running. "Looks like a quick stop," I said mostly to myself.

"Should we follow her in?" Madeline asked.

"Not just yet. I'd say she's not planning on staying too long." Within seconds of the words leaving my lips two gun shots rang out into the night. They echoed into the silent neighborhood and both Madeline and I jumped in our seats. I reached for my door and quickly got out of the car in time to catch Alex rushing back to the cab. "Alex!" I yelled out. She paused to look in my direction, and before I knew it, she was back in the cab and sped off down the street.

"Get back in the car!" Madeline yelled.

"Go on without me," I answered. "I want to check the house."

Once again squealing her tires on the pavement, Madeline took off after the cab.

Chapter 19

I was alone and the neighborhood around me was now eerily quiet. No one seemed to wake from the sound of the gunfire, and I soon realized that in this neighborhood, it wasn't enough for anyone to call the police. Ohio City bordered some rough areas and it was possible that small arms fire was an occasional occurrence. Unfortunately, that left me alone to go search for the victim of the gun shots I had heard.

After a few minutes of talking to myself in front of Charles Beard's house, I finally had the courage to climb the porch stairs. I almost knocked on the door when I realized that if anyone was home, they were not going to be able to answer. I gave the door a try and it was locked tight, and blinds on all the windows kept me from peaking through. I tried the door one more time before moving around to the side of the wraparound porch, where I found a side door that was also locked. Alex must have gone around back because she would not have had time to lock up the house when she left. Side steps took me off the porch and onto a gravel driveway. I looked into the garage windows noticing only a small car parked inside. I followed a well-groomed stone path into the backyard where it opened into a small, manicured garden, complete with a bird bath. A undersized landing off of the house led down to the garden, and as I turned to go up I noticed the backdoor was wide open.

Proceeding slowly up the stairs and into the house, I realized that Alex had covered a lot of ground from the time I heard the shots to when I saw her running towards the cab. The house was completely black and I used a tissue from my pocket to fumble for a light switch on the wall. Track lighting came on, illuminating a very modern kitchen which seemed out of place in the old house.

"Hello," I yelled for some unknown reason. "Is anyone home?" It just seemed right to ask. No one responded leaving me more worried about what I was going to find. Slowly, I made my way through the dining room and into the living room where I found the staircase leading up to the second floor. Gravitating towards the first step, I hesitated as I noticed a room off of a small hall on the other side of the stairs. A table lamp was casting light across the walls and hardwood floor, slowly changing the shadows as I walked towards it. Before I even walked into Charles Beard's study I knew what I was about to find, as I could see a pair of feet sticking out from the doorway. Poking my head inside, I wished I hadn't, as I caught sight of the remains of Mr. Beard.

There had been two shots to the head, at close range, with a medium caliber weapon. One shot took off half his face and the other came in right on target. It was hard to tell because so little was left, most of it having been shot off onto the bookshelf behind him. The hit looked sloppy and quickly done. The kill was not clean.

Finishing my quick inspection of the body, I stepped over Beard and went to his desk carefully searching for the evidence against Chelsea. The desk was clean and I scanned the bookshelves trying to find a safe or some other hiding place he might have had. I came up empty but I was expecting that. Alex would never have put herself in this situation without at least getting what she came for. At least now I knew that we were after the same thing, but what I still couldn't figure out was why. I thought about turning on the computer and searching its files, but unfortunately my skills were lacking, and I had to assume that any evidence was well hidden and password-protected......a job for someone else.

I made my way back through the house turning off lights and trying not to disturb anything. I left the backdoor open just as I had found it and walked down the driveway to the front sidewalk. I pulled out my cell phone and dialed Colin's number.

"It's late, what do you want?" His voice sounded like he had actually been asleep.

"I've got something for you."

"That girl didn't try to kill you did she?"

"No, but she might have shot Charles Beard."

"You don't say." Now he was awake. "How do you know this?"

"Long story. Meet me over at the diner across from the market on West 25th. Buy me a coffee and a corned beef sandwich while I explain it to you. Also send some of your boys to Beard's place to clean up the mess in his study."

"Are you there now?"

"Just leaving. I'm on foot so give me a few minutes to get out of here before you call in the cavalry."

"Alright, let me throw some clothes on and I'll meet you at the diner." Colin hung up.

I put my phone back into my pocket and walked in the shadows of the night towards West 25th Street. The wind blew and rattled the branches leaving a coolness in the air that we hadn't had all summer. The smell of rain was coming across the breeze from the lake and the thought of a killer on the loose had me quicken my step as I made my way to the diner.

Chapter 20

Shit, this wasn't good, Alex thought. *What the hell had Jack been doing at Beard's house?*

"Got someone following us, Miss," the taxi driver said as he maneuvered the cab through nearly empty streets.

"What?" Alex turned to see a silver Mercedes a block behind them. "There's an extra hundred in it if you lose them."

"Not a problem. Ah Miss."

"What now?"

"Could those have been gun shots I heard coming from the house a few minutes ago?"

"Another hundred and you didn't hear a thing."

"Got a pretty good memory it's always been a fault of mine."

"How convenient, three hundred to lose the tail and have some friggin' memory loss."

"Sounds good Miss."

The little bastard was pretty brave to try and take her for more money. How did he know she wouldn't shoot him dead in his own filthy cab? What a mess the night had become. Jack Francis could become a real problem if she left him to it. The man had made the first half of the night pretty enjoyable. Dinner had been nice and dessert back at his place even better. She would have liked to enjoyed him one more time, but now, well that probably was out. Why did he have to be so damn curious and follow her?

"I think I lost that Mercedes Miss," the cabby called back over his shoulder.

It had been a Mercedes hadn't it, a silver one with a black convertible if she was correct. She only had a brief look at the thing but Alex had no doubt about what she saw. That car did not belong to Jack so someone else was tailing her. There always was the chance that Jack was with them but that still left another person involved tonight. Silver Mercedes, Alex thought, who could it be? Who else was connected and drove a silver Mercedes convertible? Those damn brats, the Gilmore sisters, that's who drove that car. Jack must have been hired by the old man and now one of the girls was tagging along. It had to be the older one, since Alex doubted the old man was going to let his youngest go running around town in the middle of the night after everything she had been through. Besides the oldest, Madeline, yeah that was her name, was always flaunting herself around the casino. She would probably enjoy Jack's company. Alex certainly had.

"Take me to the Arcade," she told the driver. The cab could leave her there in front of the hotel and she could easily grab another one home. Alex had no desire to let the driver know where she lived in case he got the idea to swindle more money from her. Better to let him believe she was staying at the hotel than allow him another chance to profit from her activities tonight.

Alex reached for her purse as the cab pulled up in front of the Arcade. She handed the driver three one hundred-dollar bills.

"Hey, what about money for the fare?" the cabby hollered.

"I think you have plenty there," Alex said nodding to the money she had handed him.

She got out of the cab in front of the hotel and reached into her purse for her cell phone. Quickly she dialed Lee Kershaw's phone number from memory, but he must have had his phone off because it went right to voicemail without a single ring.

"Lee," Alex began to leave a message, "I was just followed by one of the sisters involved in our antique affair. Could you please look into this for me and get back to me soon with any information." She hoped he was smart enough to figure out what she meant and needed. Too many details should never be left on a message but she needed Kershaw to work on this right away.

Chapter 21

Soft and calm, the voice on the other end of the line was in control. There was a hint of an accent to it, maybe East European. None of these things bothered Lee Kershaw as much as the raspy coldness that also came when the man spoke. Kershaw had never seen the man's face and he had no desire to. His voice was enough to keep him away but it was his indifference towards human life that really bothered him.

"As I have told you before," the man continued, "I am already employed at the moment."

"It is important for me to have this done and as always you will be paid well."

"I never overextend myself Mr. Kershaw. When one does this they lose their edge."

"But this concerns the incompleteness of your last task for me. I need a more thorough job done."

"I believe that is an insult Mr. Kershaw. My last job was completed as you requested."

"It was not you that failed."

"I am aware of your predicament," the man's voice was cold and steady "and because I am aware of your predicament, I will listen to your proposal. So please continue."

"It is about the job at the Zeitlin place."

"Yes, and I cleaned up after the Italian hack you had sent in there before me."

"And it was done very well." Now Kershaw was kissing a little butt to stroke the man's ego. "But the problem now is with the girl."

"She is not of my concern. I would not have been so daft as to leave her alive in the first place."

"I understand, but our Italian friend was not as wise." He was right, Kershaw thought. If he had sent him in the first place none of this would have happened.

"A genetic fault of his, the man was stupid at birth."

"Anyways, she was the younger of Captain Gilmore's two daughters, as I am sure you know. However, my problem is with the older girl, Madeline. She has decided to become involved with her sister's troubles and is finding her nose where it doesn't belong.

Becoming too nosey for her own good you might say." Kershaw paused giving the man a chance to speak.

"Go on Mr. Kershaw. Ask me what it is you want. I'm still listening."

Kershaw felt by the man's voice that he was already planning. He worked that way and was a cunning adversary. *Thank God he is on my payroll*, Kershaw thought. "All I need is a warning. Something to let the Gilmores know it's time to back off. Can you handle it for me?"

"Fortunately for you Mr. Kershaw my current state of employment puts me in a perfect position to accomplish such a persuasion for you."

"Really, who are you working for?"

"Do not insult me with such questions as the answers are none of your concern."

"I apologize, it was simple conversation."

"If you will please send the funds to my normal account we can go forth in the matter. Rest assured that once I receive the money what you have asked of me will be completed."

"It will be sent immediately."

"Mr. Kershaw, your business is always appreciated. You may consider this matter resolved." The phone went silent.

Alex's message on Kershaw's phone had not hinted at any decisive action, but with so much already going wrong he was not taking any chances. The man's voice was intimidating and his actions towards the Gilmores would be as well. Kershaw knew he should have sent him from the beginning and if he had, the situation would have never had progressed this far. Jimmy DeLuca would never have been there to screw up and Chelsea Gilmore would now be dead. Another drugged up debutante forgotten.

Chapter 22

The coffee was strong and bitter, perfect. The potatoes were lacking seasoning and seemed to have dried out under the heat lamps, yet the diner managed some of the juiciest and most tender corned beef I've ever had. If I ever came back for another meal it would be coffee and corned beef only because nothing else was needed. One bite of that corned beef and all the sins of the awful potatoes were suddenly forgiven. It was too bad Colin's tardiness would not be.

I had been stuck here stewing for over an hour now. Add that to my walk time and it had been an hour and a half of waiting for his lethargic ass. I had walked a good ten blocks on an increasingly windy night after seeing a man's brains cover his bookshelf. If Colin had the nerve to fall back asleep I would kill him. My phone rattled in my pocket. "That better be him," I thought out loud.

"You still there?" Colin asked.

"Where else would I be? I'm in a back booth waiting for you."

"I'm walking in now." The phone clicked off and a minute later Colin stormed in through the front door with a sense of urgency. He flopped down in the booth across from me and gave a sigh as the waitress came over. She pushed a coffee in front of him and tried to hand him a menu but he waved it off. "I'm not eating but thanks."

"Where have you been?" I asked sounding a little stressed and in need of some bourbon.

"Well, I was asleep so I had to get dressed. Katya had gotten home from work a few minutes before you called and I had to explain to her why I was dashing off in the middle of the night. On my way here I called the Cleveland Police with information of a shooting at Beard's. Funny that no one else in the neighborhood had called. No reports of gunfire or anything."

"The shooting of Beard," I stressed.

"I told them I had information from an anonymous source that they would find Beard dead inside."

"I'm a little surprised no one in the neighborhood bothered to report the shooting."

"It doesn't matter, a black and white made the trip over to check the place out."

"And..."

"And," Colin continued, "you need to stop interrupting me."

"Sorry I'm a little impatient it's been a long night."

"Private practice has made you soft. You didn't used to be so jumpy."

"I was mentally prepared for nights like these back when I was with the Bureau, and in the Army I was too young to worry. The whole young and invincible thing I guess. Are you going to continue or are we talking about my psyche all night?"

"Sorry, well just so you know I think you better get your mind prepared because your night is going to get longer."

"Great," I should have seen it coming. "What is it?"

"The house was clean."

"Impossible the guy's brains were all over the place. Shit half his face was blown off."

"Black and white found the back door wide open checked through the house and found no one home."

"How long from when I left until the local boys got there?" Surprisingly I regained my composure pretty quickly.

"Hour if I had to guess. Not enough time to get a body out and clean the place up."

"Apparently it is."

"You know," Colin started, "if the same thing hadn't happened at the Zeitlin place I would have swore you'd gone crazy. Hallucinating and such."

"Wish I had. I wonder what happened to Alex."

"Madeline lost her." I looked at him quizzically. "She called me since she didn't have your number. She does now by the way."

"Great. Where's she at now?"

"I sent her home. She wanted to meet up with us but I told her to stay out of the whole mess."

"She won't," I said. "That woman is driven. She spent all night following Alex and me."

"You know Jack after all these years you still amaze me. You are with two women tonight and one's a killer while the other is a stalker. I can't imagine how you find them but you sure can pick the good ones." Colin had the audacity to laugh at himself.

"Really funny, in fact I'm not sure if either is true yet."

"I suggest you figure it out quickly before you find yourself in real trouble with one or the other or both."

"You must mean more trouble and don't forget for a second that you are the reason I'm in this mess."

"That's why I'm here watching over you."

"Thanks," I said. "Thanks a lot."

Chapter 23

My few hours of sleep were incredibly restless as I tossed and turned in my bed. I finally got out of bed determined not to fight it any longer. Even with the case on my mind all night, I had been unable to come up with a way to proceed now that Charles Beard was dead. The problem was I had no way of proving that either. I guess the best I could do was prove that he was missing. As with any problem I get stuck on, I needed to look for a distraction. Problems faced head on can be stubborn and unrelenting so I decided to clear my mind of the road blocks.

The cab ride east down Euclid Avenue barely took ten minutes before I found myself hopping out on Mayfield Road in Little Italy. I ducked into Corbo's Bakery for a cup of coffee and some fresh biscotti. It was still early but the day was giving every indication of heat and humidity. The wind was still blowing, and the smell of rain continued to linger in the air, but somehow a muggy day was upon me. I took my breakfast to go and walked slowly over to University Circle and into the Cleveland Museum of Art, in search of some air conditioning and a little piece of mind. I have wasted hours in this museum, usually as a distraction for a cold winter day. The Cleveland Museum of Art has the size and beauty of any major art venue in the country, and Gilded Age wealth had left collections that could compete with New York and Chicago, while steady donations had allowed the museum to grow over the years. I had full hope that a few restful hours inside would make everything right with the world.

I had knocked out all of my favorite collections finishing up with the medieval armory, and as I decided to take a quick stroll around Wade Lake, I felt someone coming up behind me. I assumed it was another museum guest, looking over my shoulder at the antique guns, when I heard a calm, sultry voice that I was not expecting.

"A room full of weapons created for some of the cruelest paths to death and now we worship them as art. We humans are a romantic species wouldn't you say?" I turned to look right into Alex's eyes, her soft pouty lips, and realized I now had two women following me. My eyes darted around the large marble room anticipating Madeline's arrival as well. "I can see the cat has got your tongue this morning," Alex continued.

"Your appearance is a little unexpected, considering last night. Did you come here looking for some piety?"

"No I prefer facing my problems head on and by myself."

"And I'm a problem?" I asked.

"Yet to be determined Jack. Why did you follow me last night?"

"Why did you shoot Charles Beard?" I had run out of patience for games and I wanted to get right to the point. Her reaction and response would tell me a lot about her and the truth.

"So he's dead then?"

She seemed honestly shocked but I was not going to give in so easily. "Don't play coy with me Alex. I watched you head towards his house seconds before I heard gunfire and then you came running out at full speed."

"Did you actually see me go into his house?"

I started to think about her question, but before I could give her an honest answer, she continued, "I don't believe you did Jack."

"I did see Charles Beard's dead body."

"Well good for you." She was still so calm. She radiated with a confidence that fueled her sexuality. "I seemed to have missed the shooting on the morning news. You did remember to call the police and report it?

"The body went missing." I was a little ashamed to admit it even though it was out of my hands.

There was a small moment of shock on her face, or possibly confusion. "Were you able to recover what you were looking for then?"

I knew I had already given her too much, but in reality, I had already gone too far by sleeping with her. All hell, what did I care? "No, that seems to have gone missing as well."

"Funny," was the only response she had. "Good day Jack, and take care of yourself." She turned to go down the white, marble staircase that led to the lawn surrounding Wade Lake. "Oh, one more thing Jack."

"What is it?"

"I would just hate it if you thought I killed that man."

"I'm not sure what to think Alex," and I walked away before anymore could be said.

Chapter 24

Chelsea was sound asleep in bed when Madeline returned home. She had a bottle of sleeping pills on the table next to her, and the TV was muted. In the glow of the TV light, Madeline could make out streaks under Chelsea's eyes where her makeup had run. Even though it seemed like her little sister had gone to bed upset, Madeline took a minute to enjoy the rare silence. She hadn't talked to Chelsea all night and Madeline wondered if that was to blame for how rough Chelsea looked.

She slept very little that night and more than once had thought of taking a few of Chelsea's sleeping pills. A dance had played out between Jack Francis and Charles Beard. Madeline could feel a fondness for Jack developing. He was a handsome man with the right mix of confidence and compassion. The night had nearly reached a boiling point for Madeline when she watched him take Alex up to his condo, but she had calmed her nerves. She always got what she wanted eventually.

Then there was Charles Beard, that scum of a man who had the audacity to blackmail her sister. Part of her hoped that Alex had shot him dead, as it would have been one useful purpose to that woman's life. Yet if she did shoot Beard then Alex more than likely had her hands on the blackmail evidence, which according to Madeline, put her right back into the frying pan.

There were unseen forces at play here but the problem was Madeline had no sense of what they could be. First off, who had shot the man in the photos with Chelsea and who would have left her alive to see it? Maybe her sister was being set up to cause the family embarrassment? Alex was somehow connected to the shooting, she could figure that much out. It would explain why she was at Beard's store and at his house. Did Alex's shooting of Charles Beard rule out the possibility that the whole episode was blackmail from the beginning or a mere coincidence? There was no such thing as coincidences, Madeline thought, and if Beard was involved from the beginning, then why kill him now? Alex must have shot Beard tonight to retrieve the evidence of the first murder, therefore, Beard was outside of the original plan. He stumbled upon Chelsea by accident and then took advantage of the situation. That had to be it, but unfortunately it led Madeline down another road.

Jack and Madeline both saw Alex head towards Beard's house tonight, and Alex had seen Jack before she took off back to the cab after the gunfire. Madeline had tailed Alex in her car afterward, and if Alex knew she was being followed, and had identified her car, she would know she had been there too. The thought worried her because she knew Alex had no qualms about killing Beard to cover up a murder, so why would she hesitate in doing it again? Then the worst thought of the night hit her. There had been two witnesses to the first murder, and Alex had shot the first one tonight. The second one was sleeping in her bedroom down the hall. Chelsea was in danger.

Madeline needed composure and she needed a plan. Talking through all of this with Jack might help. He may even have a good idea about how to protect Chelsea. The man was former FBI after all. She had to rely on herself first and foremost though. It was Madeline's job to look after her sister and she would do whatever was needed to see her safe. Now was the time to act, and no longer react, to what was happening.

Chapter 25

"We need to talk," ordered Madeline over the phone. I immediately regretted Colin giving her my number. Sure it was a public number, and she could have found it on her own, but Colin made it too easy for her.

"About what?" I had a pretty good idea that any further interaction outside of my condo would not be wise today, especially after the run-in at the museum.

"Can we at least meet for dinner and talk about it in person? I'm not a big fan of this over the phone chit-chat."

"I don't know it's already been a really long day."

"I promise not to shoot anybody unlike your more recent date." The woman had a little acid in her voice but it was quickly covered by a casual laugh.

"I'm still under the employment of your father. Do you really think it is a good idea to meet in such a social manner?" I could have cared less about what old man Gilmore thought, but I was looking for any excuse not to meet her for dinner. I was staying home and staying out of trouble.

"That's a bullshit excuse and you know it Jack. Dinner will be about the job you're doing for Father anyway. Meet me at the club at 7:00. I'll be at the bar." She hung up not even giving me a chance to respond.

I put my phone down on the bar in front of me and took a sip of my bourbon. Katya was standing on the other side with her arms crossed. Her eyes were boring a hole in my forehead as I sensed her staring at me. Looking up was a mistake, just another in a long list of them I had been making lately. She pounced the minute we made eye contact.

"You be careful with that one. Madeline will have your mind warped in no time. Oh, don't give me that look Jack. I know you are a sucker for a beautiful woman and this one is rich and smart to boot. Sometimes a little too smart for her own good."

"What do you want me to do? She wasn't taking no for an answer. I really just wanted to go home, plop my ass down on the couch, and call it a day."

"No one tells Madeline Gilmore anything, especially no. The smart thing would have been to not answer the phone."

"Hell why didn't you tell me that before I picked it up? A little bit of help from you might have allowed me to avoid dinner tonight."

"Jack, what do you want me to do hold your hand? Sometimes you're a smart boy, and other times you're a sucker. Now listen to me, Madeline doesn't fall for men. Every man in her life is an object to use to her advantage. She will eat you alive if you're not careful. That woman wants something more from you and it's not a commitment." Katya was burning but she was truly worried about me.

"Wow, aren't you being a little hard on her? I thought the two of you were practically family?"

"My dad and Captain Gilmore were close but Madeline and I are not. Those two girls and I never ran in the same circles. Just because Madeline's father is my godfather never meant that she and I would become fast friends."

"It's only dinner anyways. There can't be much harm in that."

"You're being pretty optimistic. How did your date last night go?" The woman was devious and had the smile to go with it.

"Colin told you? I should have known."

"He had no choice, especially when you called to get him out of bed in the middle of the night."

"She followed me to the museum today," I blurted out.

"Who did?"

"Alex, my date from last night."

"Well how about that. That is awful brave for a woman who shot someone last night. Then again she could be a total psychopath or completely innocent. Those are only the only two options there."

"Why do you say that?" I asked.

"Well if you shoot someone and everyone knows it was you, then you go and hide. If you don't, then you are obviously too messed up in the head to care."

"Expert analysis again Katya," I got up to leave the bar but turned back. "If she didn't shoot him then who did?"

"There must be another player in the game that you are not aware of."

"I was afraid you'd say that."

"Oh Jack."

"Yeah?"

"Have fun on your little date tonight."

"Thanks. By the way, Madeline told me to meet her at the club. Which club might that be?"

"Only one she would go to for dinner. Erieview Tower top floor and don't bother taking your wallet, you can't afford it."

"Thanks for the vote of confidence. See you later."

Katya answered, "Anytime," as I walked out.

Chapter 26

I found myself deep in thought as I dressed for dinner with Madeline. My nerves were a little on edge and not from anticipation of my date but because of my conversation with Katya. Had my instincts told me that Alex was the one who shot Charles Beard, then I think I would have been alright, but somewhere inside it felt like she was innocent and that was the problem. The mere thought of an unknown player had me worried. The case had me in the dark as it was, and I had no desire to find out things were going to get even more complicated.

Also, there were the missing bodies. It was an oddity that at least made some sense, no bodies, then no witnesses, then no murder. There were still two witnesses for those missing bodies, and so there was still a pair of murders to solve. Chelsea and I were the two remaining witnesses to two murders, and neither of us actually saw the murder only the aftermath. Where did that put us? At risk? Probably.

Assuming that Alex was after the same photos of Chelsea that I was, I had to assume she was either working for Captain Gilmore, or whoever killed the first man. It was doubtful Captain Gilmore had hired two people for the same job, so Alex was working for the opposition or at least connected to them, but who were they? Based on my own assumptions, Alex had every reason to want Charles Beard dead, because it would make confiscating the photos from him easier, and also eliminate a prime witness to the first murder. Even with all reasoning pointing to Alex as the shooter, my gut told me otherwise.

Had I been blinded by the woman's charm in one quick evening? I doubt it. My life had been mostly spent alone and independent. Sure, I relied on a solid group of guys in my Army days, and even now with my FBI time behind me, Colin was still a constant in my life. He had been a good partner and a reliable friend. My parents had passed away a few years back and my only disappointment was that they never saw me married. It was in the love department I often found myself alone. Military, then FBI lifestyles, had allowed me very little time to nurture any relationships. Now that I have retired to the private sector, I have found it hard to abandon old ways. My independence has allowed me to deflect every woman I have come across and now Alex was going to change that in one night? I found it very doubtful in deed. My gut was right and there was no way I was blinded.

There was another factor telling me Alex was innocent. She had the appearance of hired help. The woman was too cool, too calm, and fully in control of herself. It told me she was not the shooter at the Zeitlin house trying to cover her own tracks. No, she was hired to clean up someone else's mess. If Alex hadn't done the first shooting, then Katya was right about another player but now I was wondering if there were two? Had there been two separate murderers, one for each body?

I toiled with every scenario as I finished getting dressed and drove over to the Erieview Tower. I nearly ran over the valet as I pulled up to the building because I was so deep in thought. Inside, the lobby of the skyscraper was nearly empty. A cavernous corridor filled with quiet echoes of a long work day gone by. Toward the bank of the elevators, a security desk sat aglow from the monitors, illuminating a lone man guarding the post.

He looked at me with warring eyes as I approached him. "I'm heading up to the club," I said to him, looking for a little help with directions. The security guard simply pointed to the elevator closest to his desk and I headed into it. There were no buttons for individual floors, but instead the gold panel simply had an intercom button, and a spot to slide a magnetic card. An engraved gold plated sign told me to use the intercom if I was not a club member.

A voice crackled over the speaker as I waited, and the elevator closed off from the world. "How may I help you tonight sir?" I looked over my shoulder at a mounted camera.

I was amused already and I still had to get into the club. "I'm supposed to be meeting with Madeline Gilmore."

"One moment please."

I waited patiently for about thirty seconds before the elevator began to move upward. The steel car moved quickly up the length of the tower to the top floor, where the doors opened onto a marble floor and well groomed maître d'. Behind the club's greeter was a floor to ceiling view of downtown Cleveland, and the evening lights sparkled through the windows. What a view.

"Miss Gilmore is in the bar waiting for you sir," the maître d' pointed off to his right.

"Thank you."

"Will you please inform Miss Gilmore her table is available whenever she is ready."

"I can do that," but I had been dismissed as the maître d' pretended to busy himself. Gypsy in the palace, I thought to myself as I walked into the bar feeling a little out of place.

Chapter 27

The bar lacked the ambience of a country club that I was expecting to see. Instead the room had a more modern flair. Glass windows lined three of the walls giving views of the sprawling city lights and the harbor to the north. Rather than the standard cocktail tables there were clusters of sofas and armchairs, set up to compliment an array of coffee tables. Candles were lit across the room giving a warm feel to the openness of the room.

On the fourth wall a sleek, stone bar with a dark marble top was highlighted by lights from the floor. More candles along the bar top flickered light around the cocktail glasses served to members and their guests. The wall behind the bar had a series of steps lined with an assortment of liquor bottles, and a waterfall ran down each step. It gave the effect of the liquor bottles floating on water. Small lights illuminated each bottle from below, calling for each one to be tasted.

The opulence of the place would have normally made me a little awestruck, but there was something truly more beautiful at the bar. Madeline stood to greet me as I drew close and I was instantly speechless by her appearance. Long, tan legs climbed into the sky until they were concealed by a short, black cocktail dress. Bare shoulders led to a soft neck calling out to be kissed, and a blue diamond necklace draped into her chest becoming lost in her bosom. More diamonds dangled from her ears, and fought for attention with the sparkles in her eyes. The strawberry blonde hair I first saw in a ponytail was now done up like Oscar Night with not one strand out of place. As Madeline came close to me and as we greeted, I noticed every eye in the room had turned to watch her.

"Jack," she said applying a soft hug and kiss along my cheek. "I'm glad to see you made it. Please come have a seat."

"The man up front asked me to tell you your table is ready."

"We're in no hurry. Stephan will hold the table all night for me if I asked him to."

"Stephan?"

"The maître d'. He's been here for as long as I can remember. Come on now, sit and have a drink."

I sat down next to Madeline, feeling the eyes of the room upon us. While I struggle to find the right words, distracted by Madeline's beauty, the Filipino bartender set a Pappy Van Winkle in front of me before I even had a chance to order. "You're on your game," I said to Madeline.

"It really was nothing. I remembered you were drinking it when you came to the house to speak with father."

"So you really did catch the whole conversation?"

"The whole thing," she smiled.

"In that case would you like to tell me why I'm here tonight?"

"No, not quite yet. We will save our business for dinner. For now let's sit, unwind, and enjoy each other's company." Madeline patted my thigh for a second and then added another smile to the mix.

It seemed like she was working me and I was beginning to believe Katya's warning about her. A beautiful, smart woman who used every man she came across, now that was a deadly combination. Was I about to be used? With one look at Madeline, part of me didn't really care. Besides, it couldn't possibly end any worse than my night with Alex had.

Chapter 28

When dinner arrived, so did the business part of our conversation. In front of me sat a plate of medium rare, Colorado lambs chops, with an ample amount of morel mushrooms, and fingerling potatoes, drizzled with white truffle oil. I sure hoped whatever Madeline was going to say would not ruin my appetite.

"I want to talk to you about your new friend Alex. There is something very fishy about her involvement in all of this."

"Tell me about it," I said with a mouthful of lamb. "She followed me to the art museum today. I was half expecting you to jump out from behind the Monet." I laughed. She didn't.

"A little brave after last night don't you think? What did she want from you?"

"I'm not really sure, the whole thing was a bit weird. It was as if she wanted to proclaim her innocence but she never came out and said it."

"Was that it?"

"Pretty much." I kept it short not wanting to share too much right away. I still had no idea what Madeline wanted from me, if anything, and the food in front of me was bound to get cold if I told the whole recap of the morning's events. "So what else do you have for me?"

"There is nothing really new to tell you. It is more like a few things running around my head that I wanted to get out."

"Shoot."

"OK," Madeline started, "if Alex shoots Beard, why?"

"She was after the same things we were."

"Exactly, but why?"

"Could she be working for your father?"

"I don't think so." For Madeline this clearly was not a possibility.

"Neither do I, which means she is working for someone else. If my assumptions are correct then that party would be the one who shot the man in those photos with Chelsea."

"What if Alex did the first shooting too?"

"I'm not seeing it. Call it a gut instinct if you will, but Alex has hired help written all over her."

"Yeah she does," Madeline smirked. "Do you think she did Beard then?"

"Right now she is the only suspect we've got," I said tossing back the last few morels on my plate. "But then again we don't have a body either."

"You didn't answer my question. What does your all-knowing instinct tell you? Did she shoot Beard?"

"My instinct tells me there is more here than Alex shooting Beard, and whether she shot him or not, we have another problem to worry about."

"And what might that be?" I noticed Madeline had managed to finish her dinner of butter-poached walleye, fennel slaw, and Tuscan potatoes, even while talking. I looked her over and wondered where she managed to put it.

"The problem is that even if Alex did shoot Beard, there is still another party involved and that party now has Beard's blackmail evidence on your sister. The same party has killed a witness to one murder already, but there are still two other witnesses out there."

"I don't quite follow."

"Your sister may not remember seeing any shooting but she sure did see the corpse—a corpse which has disappeared and probably for good reason. The second witness is me and I'm in the same boat as Chelsea. I may have not seen Charles Beard get shot but I sure as hell saw what was left of him before his remains disappeared too."

"If I am following you correctly," Madeline said, "then Chelsea is in danger still."

"All I am saying is there is someone out there going to a lot of trouble to cover up these killings, and so far they've been able to keep them off the public radar. Needless to say I have to believe they are going to try and tie up all their loose ends."

"Meaning, as I said before, Chelsea is in danger."

"Meaning Chelsea and I might be in danger," Saying it out loud struck a chord inside of me and for the first time in a while, I was a little worried. "Someone should be looking after your sister, and Madeline, you may want to reconsider getting involved."

Chapter 29

Outside the Erieview Tower a man waited in the dark and watched as the valet pulled a silver Mercedes around to the front. Leaping from the car, the young man ran back towards the garage quickly. He smiled to himself amused at the predictability of people, and then made his way to the Mercedes. The doors had been left unlocked and he slipped into the cramped back seat, waiting silently in the dark for his prey. He laughed to himself in silence as he noticed the keys still in the ignition. He had come prepared to bypass the locks on his own but the valet had made it just a little easier. Slouching down further into the shadows of the rear seat he waited silently as he watched the valet come back, driving Jack Francis's Austin Healy.

Madeline and Jack had made their way down from dinner, and now stood in the night saying their goodbyes. There was a kiss on the cheek and a hug lasting a little too long. Jack was in his car first as

Madeline stood chatting with the valet. The man watched as Jack rolled down his window to speak to Madeline, and then was waved off by a kiss blown in his direction. He watched as Jack's Austin Healy pulled around a corner and was out of sight. A minute later Madeline tipped the young valet as he opened her door for her. The engines in the German car came alive, and the man sat still in the shadows of the back seat until they were a few blocks away from the club.

"Good evening Madeline," the soft and raspy voice came from the back seat. Madeline screamed as she slammed on the brakes forcing the man to jerk forward in his seat. When the tires and Madeline both stopped screeching, the man spoke again. "The alley over on the right looks like a good place to talk, Madeline, and we do need to talk." He watched her search her rear-view for him but the shadows concealed his face. Giving up, she stayed silent and pulled into the alley slowly, hoping someone would see her. The man could see she was obviously shaken as he looked across her bare, tense shoulders. If he had been a man without control the beautiful woman would have been taken right there in the car, but he had learned a long time ago that primordial urges led to sloppiness and sloppiness would always get you caught.

"What do you want?" Madeline was finally able to get out of her mouth as she stopped the car in the alley.

"Just to talk. Now pull up a little further dear, this is going to be a private conversation." She moved the car a little further into the alley and he noticed her chill as her body stiffened. His voice had that effect on people. His calmness told them who was in control. The raspy sound, mixed with an indistinguishable hint of a European accent, something he had worked hard on, for some reason brought the fear out in most people. Now it was having its way with the woman in the front seat. He was positive Madeline would be hearing his voice in her sleep tonight. That was if she could sleep at all. "This is good," he said in regards to her moving of the car. "We need to talk about your sister Chelsea. You see Madeline, your time as an amateur sleuth is over. There are certain people who do not want you snooping around anymore. My job is simply to come and ask you politely to stop." Madeline sat silently look straight ahead. "I also have to ask you to stop Mr. Francis from any further investigating as well."

"My father is paying him," the words fell out of her mouth like a child in trouble.

"I am aware of that. You will give your father this, and you will tell him of our little talk. I believe these things should be enough to have him call off Mr. Francis," and he handed Madeline an envelope from the backseat. "Fire him or pay him off, I do not care which, but all of this ends tonight."

"But what about Chelsea? She will still be in danger. We can't stop until she is safe." Madeline, normally a strong woman, was shaken and her voice revealed it.

"Chelsea is safe as long as you do as you've been told. Do you understand what I am telling you, Madeline? I would hate to have to pay you another visit."

Madeline gave a nod with her head as she softly answered, "Yes." The car door opened behind her and the man slipped out into the dark alley, never showing himself. She didn't once think about following him and it was probably best. Instead she sat there studying the envelope he had given her. With the overhead lamp turned on, she decided to open it before she got home. The envelope was sealed and she tore through it with her hands as a memory card fell out onto her lap. There was still more inside and Madeline frantically pulled out a small stack of photos. In her hands were photos of Chelsea. The photos Charles Beard had used to blackmail her sister and now Madeline had them.

Chapter 30

Out of the northeast, the wind whistled off of the lake, bringing with it some much needed cool air. Today the weather felt nice but tomorrow the rain would come. The third day of a nor'easter always brought rain.

The drive home from dinner was as painless as dinner had been. I had escaped unscathed and I couldn't wait to tell Katya. Even with all the sexual energy Madeline had brought to the table, I had kept my composure and my head. Had it been another time or place I would have done anything to bring her home with me, but not tonight. Madeline also frightened me a little. There was something about the way she handled herself. I found her to be as calculated as Alex, and after last night, maybe that's why I had veered away from Madeline.

I reached my floor and left the elevator, unlocked my front door, and entered a dark condo only lit from the street lamps beyond my windows. *I really need to start leaving a light on*, I thought to myself, as I tossed my keys on the dining room table, and navigated the place semi-blindly. Venturing into the kitchen, I finally hit a light switch, and poured myself a glass of ice with some bourbon on top. With the glass topped off, I turned back toward my living room and the light from the kitchen revealed that I was not alone.

"Be a doll and grab another glass Jack." I showed no expression, and instead I just turned back into the kitchen to pour Alex a bourbon. The women in my life were starting to no longer surprise me by their actions, and it really made me worry about where my life was heading. When I came back from the kitchen, a table lamp had been turned on and Alex sat there smiling mischievously at me. "So how was it? Come on and sit down. Tell me all about dinner will you?"

"Following me again?" I asked damn well knowing the answer.

"Let's call it keeping tabs." I handed her the drink and she sat back into her chair to get comfortable. "It must not have been as good as last night considering you came home alone."

"Actually dinner was really enjoyable." I was not about to give her any satisfaction by responding to her little comment. "What are you doing here Alex?" getting right to the point.

"We need to talk. Clear the air so to speak."

"So get to it. I don't have a lot of patience with people who have broken into my house in the middle of the night."

"Who broke in? The door was open!"

"Sure it was Alex. Now don't push me."

"Fine." She took a long pull from her drink. "I did not shoot Charles Beard. Let's just get that clear right now."

"Then who did?"

"I'm not sure."

"And I am to believe you why?"

"Believe me or not it's the truth. I had just made it up to Beard's porch when I heard the shots. The gunfire sent me running back to the cab." There was a small amount of plea in her voice begging me to believe what she was saying, and the strange thing was she sounded sincere.

"Why are you telling me this now? Why not at the museum this morning?"

"Because, first I had to decide what I was going to do about you."

Chapter 31

I was going to die. That was my first thought when Alex said she had reached a decision about me. In the end, I had known all along she would try to kill me because Colin was always right about these things. The man always had the ability to foresee my neck in the guillotine. If Alex took a shot at me right now I would be hopelessly dead with nothing but my bourbon in hand. Ever since I left the Bureau I refused to carry a gun. I had used one enough in the Army, and later with the Feds, so I had decided in my private practice to go unarmed. Big mistake, looking at it now.

My mind was starting to work itself up, trying to figure out the best way to disarm Alex if she did pull a gun on me. But instead it was Alex who disarmed me with a subtle smile, "Relax Jack, I'm not here to hurt you."

"What gave it away?"

"You tensed up like a kid who just crapped his pants."

"I knew you weren't here to hurt me."

"Oh really?"

"If you had been, I would never have known you were here in the first place."

"Probably true," Alex said.

"So what was it you had to decide about? You've got me curious now."

"I had to find out what type of guy you really were. You seemed to have a good mind between your ears but I needed to find out how you played the game."

"And what did you find?" I asked interested to see where this was all leading.

"From what everyone says, you appear to be a straight shooter. You do a job and you do it well, but your weakness is you have morals."

"I don't see how that is a weakness."

"For some it is, but it's what I was looking for."

"If morals were what you were looking for, then where does that leave us?"

"To the point where you may be the only one I can trust, Jack."

"I'm not following Alex. Why would I be the only one?"

"You see I am the third notch on a very dirty totem pole. The man who hired me was hired by another man first."

"Who was it?"

"Not important right now," Alex continued. "The initial job seemed to go off without a hitch, or so my employer thought."

"Until Beard showed up with the photos of Chelsea."

"Right."

"And you were hired to recover those photos."

"Also right."

"OK Alex, now tell me something I don't know."

"Well, I have a problem the way I see it. Beard is dead, the evidence I was hired to retrieve is still out there, and worst of all, I was setup to look like Beard's killer."

"You still could be."

"Exactly my point. Someone wants me to look guilty."

"OK let's say I believe you were set up, then the next question is why."

"There was only one person who knew I was going to Beard's the other night and his motivation would be to close up the whole affair. Eliminate Beard as a witness, recover the evidence of the first murder, and present me as Beard's killer. Looks pretty open and shut to me."

"What about a killer for the first murder?"

"I thought you had a brain between those ears, Jack. There is no first murder. No one's called it in because no one has found a body. The only evidence out there was Beard and his camera. By what happened the other night everything gets wrapped up nicely."

"Almost, Chelsea is still out there. There is also the fact that Beard's body went missing too, so either your wrong or another hand is at play here."

"Either way, do you see now why I have no one to trust but you?" Alex pleaded.

"If you trust me, then you need to give me something to work with."

"What's that?"

"Who hired you?"

"My direct employer is a man named Lee Kershaw."

"What about the person who hired him in the first place?"

"I don't know for sure who it is. I could take a good guess but I won't until I can find out for sure."

"Not even to point me in the right direction?"

"Sorry Jack. Kershaw is what I can give you and he will be plenty to get you started. Are you starting to believe in my innocence a little bit more yet?"

"Maybe, but what now?"

"You look into Kershaw. What kind of investigator are you with a silly question like that?"

I smiled at her with my own mischievous grin. "No Alex, I meant what now, tonight?"

"Oh, well in that case it's bedtime." Alex got up and walked towards my bedroom shaking her hips softly as she moved. She looked back over her shoulder and with an inviting glance asked, "Aren't you coming with me?" Without hesitation I followed her in.

Chapter 32

By morning the weather had changed, waking me earlier than I would have liked. My windows were alive with noise as the rain danced across the glass, and the howling wind from the lake caused each pane to vibrate with the sounds of a mistuned orchestra. The only nice thing about waking up was Alex asleep next to me. I was a little surprised she had stayed the whole night, as I glanced across her soft skin, traveling along her shoulders and down to her thigh barely covered by my sheets. In the end she must have thought it better to stay than to run off again in the middle of the night. Last time it had gotten her into nothing but trouble. I left her there to sleep as I slid out of bed and tiptoed my way into the kitchen to make some coffee. The weather had really turned to shit overnight and as I glanced out my kitchen window, I hoped it was not a reflection of how my day was going to turn out.

With the coffee made I began to fry some eggs and thought about my conversation with Alex the night before. I had let her back in my bed so I must have believed in her innocence or I was just the dumbest man in the world. No, I was almost positive she had nothing to do with Charles Beard being shot. Her theory on being set up had too many holes for me though. If the plan had been to make it look like she murdered Beard then why go through all the trouble of cleaning up the body. Something told me that Alex being on Beard's porch at the wrong time was a simple coincidence. Either that or my instincts were way off and I had gone to bed with a killer last night. It would be my luck.

Every event, every scenario we discussed, every little thing led back to one thing and that was the first shooting. The first shooting was the single event which started the landslide. Whatever the motive was for the first killing it was the single thing I needed to solve. The problem was, I was nowhere near figuring it out. I had to assume— bad idea —that Chelsea's and Beard's involvement were an accident. Their involvement had sent everything into a tailspin and the rest was nothing more than a massive attempt at a coverup. It also meant that whoever had the motive for the first killing was powerful enough to move the rest of the chess pieces while being able to protect their own identity. There was one person at the top controlling all the players, or at least most of them.

The key to solving the riddle was to look closely at it from the very beginning, and that's what I was going to do. The problem was I really had no idea how I was going to do such a thing. There was a complete lack of physical evidence, Beard was dead, and the only person left to talk to was Chelsea. It was a shame Captain Gilmore had ruled her off limits from the very moment he hired me. Maybe Madeline could ask her a few questions. That might tell me something but only after I sorted through the answers she brought back to me. Then again, I really doubted Chelsea's intoxicated mind would be able to remember much about that night. There was another link to the first murder, and she was sleeping in my bed. Alex was a pawn on the chess board being manipulated in order to cover up a killer's identity.

My eggs had finished and I was stacking bacon on a plate, when Alex came out of the bedroom in the shirt I had worn last night to dinner. Her hair was disheveled and her eyes told me she was still only half-awake. She looked innocent and fragile at the moment, the opposite of the face she normally wore. A half attempt at a morning smile only added to the appearance. God, I hoped I was right about her.

"Good morning. Did you sleep alright?" I asked.

"I slept really well actually, and with the rain coming down this morning, I just wanted to stay in bed all day."

"You could have."

"Not with the smell of bacon and coffee floating through the house."

I quickly poured her a cup and made her a plate of food. "Here you go."

"Oh it's just like the Ritz."

"Not quite but I try."

"You've done wonderful," and she reached over and gave me a peck on the cheek.

"Alex, I've been thinking."

"We are going to start off the morning like this, right back to business."

"Sorry but some things have been running through my head all morning. It seems as much as you needed me last night..."

"You bet I did. I'm still sore."

"Come on Alex, quit joking and listen for a second."

"I'll behave now go on." She played with her eggs and looked like a scolded school girl.

"I've come to the conclusion that you may be the only lead I have to whoever is behind the first killing."

"What about the rich girl?"

"Chelsea is off limits as ordered by her old man. I'm going to need your help."

"I think I have helped enough for now. I gave you Kershaw and if anyone finds out I did, my life will be in jeopardy. Look into him before you go jumping into anything else. You may just find what you need."

"What does Kershaw have to do with the first shooting?"

"Jack, just look into him and stop asking me questions I can't answer."

"Can't or won't?"

"It's really the same thing," Alex got up and put her empty plate in the sink and poured herself some more coffee.

"Alright I get it. I'll go looking for this Kershaw character. At least now I have an excuse to go out in the rain."

"Not just yet," Alex said pulling me back toward the bedroom. I barely resisted.

Chapter 33

Madeline was shaken and in fear, constantly looking over her shoulder as she drove home. The man appearing in her backseat had made her realize how vulnerable she was. Chelsea was already in enough trouble, the last thing Madeline needed was to become an easy target for someone with a mind to hurt her or her family. All through the night she barely slept as her anxiety levels reached new heights, but when morning came, so did a sudden sense of relief. The weight of the night before had been lifted with the morning sun and the realization that her sister was now in the clear once her father called off Jack Francis.

Telling her father would be difficult because her involvement would most definitely set the old man off, but in the end it would be worth it. Jack Francis needed to be pulled off the case before he found himself in too deep. The man could cause problems and the faster her father and Jack could conclude their business the better Madeline would feel about her sister's safety. Madeline threw on her robe and raced downstairs from her room to find her father. Today everything would be over. Today her life could start down its path back to normalcy.

Nothing surprised her father and his reactions very rarely surprised Madeline anymore. In his younger years, his temper was explosive and borderline violent, but not today. His age had become a drain on his strength and his tirades aimed at his children were no longer worth the toll they would take on his body. Instead Madeline's news brought a mellow anger with a firm response, echoed with a tone of disappointment. Either the relief from the recovery of Chelsea's blackmail evidence superseded any anger over her involvement, or the Captain's energy levels were getting worse than she had thought. She would need to spend more time with him. To Madeline's surprise, she was being sent to call Jack Francis off of the hunt. Her father had Douglas draw up a check for her to give to him, and either Jack charged an enormous fee, or her father was supplying the man with plenty of incentive to back off.

With all the excitement of the morning, Madeline had almost forgotten to tell her sister the good news. She raced up the stairs leaving her father and Douglas in the study and bounded into Chelsea's room like she was eight years old. Madeline found her sister buried beneath a temple of covers. The room smelled of stale booze and clothes were thrown in disarray all over the floor. A bra hung from the end of Chelsea's bed and shoes were scattered around the room.

"Chelsea!" Madeline screamed attempting to wake up her sister. "Wake up, will you? I've got good news!" The girl did not stir and Madeline began to shake her sister to get her moving again.

"What do you want," came a worn and tired voice from somewhere below the covers.

"Chelsea wake up and listen to me. It's over. It's all over."

She was coming to now. "What do you mean it's over?"

"We've got the pictures back and even the memory disk he had them saved on," Madeline was skipping details and going straight to the point. Good news first, there was plenty of time for the details later. Chelsea sat up in her bed now. Her face appeared confused instead of joyful. Madeline wondered why for a moment and then assumed the girl was simply hung over and a little foggy still.

"But how," Chelsea asked. "Beard is dead and I thought everything else was lost."

"A man surprised me last night in my car. Scared the crap out of me but he gave me everything and told me it was over." The man did scare her and she was still frightened by the thought of him, but Madeline was not about to tell Chelsea that. What her sister needed right now was comfort and to not be sent back into a world of worry.

"How can this be?" Chelsea began to sob as she spoke. She tucked her head into her knees and began to mumble to herself. It took Madeline a moment to realize those were not tears of joy.

"Chelsea what's wrong? Aren't you relieved it's over?"

Her sister lifted her head to look at Madeline. The tears were streaming down her face causing last night's make up to smear. "Who was the man, Maddie? The man in your car, was it the man Daddy hired?"

"No it wasn't. I'm really not sure who he was Chelsea." Madeline was beginning to think her sister was putting together what she had left out. "It doesn't matter anyways, it's over now."

"It's not over. Can't you see it will never be over?" Chelsea burst into tears again throwing her head back down between her knees.

"But it is over Chelsea. We have the evidence and Beard is dead. What more is there?" Madeline knew of other possibilities but the man had promised it would be over and she wanted to believe him.

"No, no, no," Chelsea said rocking back and forth on her bed looking like a little girl woken from a nightmare. "It is all wrong. It's so wrong."

"What are you saying? I don't understand what is it that's wrong?" Chelsea continued to cry and Madeline stood in silence for a few minutes and watched her sister break down. Finally Madeline had enough, "Chelsea, are you still drunk because you're acting really weird?"

Chelsea stopped crying and slowly lifted her head to look at her sister. She was suddenly calm but still looked a mess from all the tears. Her eyes looked into Madeline's and she simply stared at her sister. "Maddie," she said to her sister, "I need to tell you something."

Chapter 34

The man had taken care of the problem with the Gilmore girl for Kershaw or at least that's what he had been told. It was a little unnerving to not have the evidence in hand, but Kershaw had confidence in him to do the job. Besides, Captain Gilmore would never leak the pictures and damage the image of his precious family. When the man called Kershaw late the night before, the sound of his voice sent chills through his bones, and not even the news of the job being finished comforted him until he had hung up the phone. Now it was time for another unpleasant phone call. At least this one would get Daniel Shaw off of his back for awhile.

He was put on hold trying to get through to the casino and became frustrated as the elevator music piped out of the receiver. The least Shaw could have done was give him the number to his direct line. No, instead he waited on hold like every other idiot in the city. Finally Kershaw heard a subtle click as the line came alive on the other end.

"This better be good," were the first words out of Daniel Shaw's mouth.

Kershaw would loved to kill the obnoxious bastard but the man paid too well and had dangerous friends. "It is good, so why don't you try to be a little cheerful for once."

"I have no reason to be cheerful with you Kershaw. You've given me nothing but headaches lately. What a mess you made by sending out that worthless piece of shit Jimmy DeLuca. Next time I send you a job to do, you either do it yourself or at least send a real man to do it."

"It was a mistake and I'm sorry, but at least everything is cleaned up now. Got it all wrapped up last night."

"Where's the evidence?"

"Destroyed," Kershaw lied.

"And the antique dealer?"

"Permanently, not a problem."

"How," Shaw asked.

"I have no idea and I'd rather not know."

"And who else knows about this?"

"Nobody important , why?" Kershaw asked, truly curious.

"Well you see I have been sent a gift, a coffee mug in fact."

"I'm sure it is nice."

"Shut up you smart ass," Shaw screamed into the phone. "Someone wrote a message on it, a threatening one, and I'm not a man who likes to be threatened!"

"I don't see how this is related."

"It was a Rock 'n' Roll Hall of Fame mug. Are you connecting the dots now?"

"It still could be something else," Kershaw said trying to find an escape. "You've made lots of enemies in the past."

"I'd say this message was pretty damn specific. Now tell me who else knows."

"Jimmy and Alex are the only two and I never told them directly. Well, I told Jimmy directly when I hired him for the first job and Alex figured it out by herself."

"That kid is a thorn in my side with his loose mouth and sloppy work ethic." Shaw fumed in silence on the line for a few seconds. "I don't think Jimmy has the gall to send me threats but he still is a liability. Find a permanent solution for the kid, will you?"

"Are you sure?"

"Positive, and no screw ups."

"Alright," Kershaw felt a little bad for the kid but he had brought it on himself. "I'll take care of it right away for you."

"Watch that Alex woman too. There is a leak somewhere that needs to be plugged and she is smart and motivated. Also keep your ears open about anyone one sending me this mug. I don't care if they're rumors I want to hear everything that's out on the street."

"Fine, but I want more money for this extra work."

"You're on thin ice already Kershaw. I'll get you your money even though I shouldn't. None of this would be necessary if you hadn't botched up the first job."

"You don't have to keep using me for your little tasks."

"Be glad I do," Shaw said with a sneer. "If I didn't have any use for you then where would that leave us?"

"I see your point. I'll take care of everything you asked and you take care of my money." By the time Kershaw finished his sentence he realized he was talking to a dead line. Daniel Shaw found new ways to irritate him every time they talked. Too bad the man was untouchable.

Chapter 35

Down the block from my condo is a great little coffee shop. It's not one of the overpriced chains you see occupying every other block, churning out calorie-ridden lattes. The coffee shop was a family run place where you were greeted with a smile by the owner, while his wife put out freshly baked goods. Nothing fancy here and yet every morning the place was packed with the same faces.

I had battled the wind and the rain to get there, only to wait under the awning outside for a chance to get in. The place was always busy but today the weather was sending everyone for coffee. When I did make it inside, I noticed Colin sitting at a small café table in his stereotypical FBI suit with extra starch, just like the Bureau wants it. He had a copy of the morning paper spread out in front of him and a tall coffee in hand. I had called Colin to meet me here for a little chat about Lee Kershaw. I figured it would be a problem tracking down any information on him and I thought some Bureau help might be useful. Alex had refused more of my attempts to pry her of information by burying herself in my bed and faking sleep. I finally raised a white flag and left her alone.

After standing in line for my black coffee and croissant, I finally joined Colin at his table. The man had the nerve to ignore me and continued to finish the article he was reading.

"Ah, I see you made it," he said, putting down the paper.

"Anything interesting?" I asked nodding towards the article.

"Quarterback controversy in Cleveland. Nothing like the start of a brand new season with the same old problems. What's going on with you?"

"I've got a name that I need you to check out."

"Got it from where?" he asked.

"Alex," I said burying my face in my coffee knowing damn well what was coming.

"The woman is trouble. I hope you're not about to tell me that you are still talking to her after the other night. Shit Jack, you are liable to end up the next person she shoots. I would be worried sick if she had stalked me to the museum."

"No, I haven't seen her. It's just a name she had mentioned in passing before and I wanted to check it out." I would have to explain everything to him later but now was not the time.

Colin's face told me he was not going to buy it. "You lying sack of..."

"Alright fine, she's at my place right now. I came home from dinner with Madeline last night and Alex was sitting in my living room."

"Good thing you didn't have Madeline with you."

"You're telling me."

"Jack you are crazier than the bum who preaches on the corner of East 3rd Street."

"I don't think she killed Beard," I blurted out trying to protest my sanity.

"So, she still stalked you to the museum and then broke into your condo."

"She said the door was open."

"Sure it was. Sometimes I can't believe the two of us are friends. She must be some kind of magician in the bedroom to have you so screwed up."

"She is." I could not help but smile.

"It frustrates me to discuss your stupidity so early in the morning. So what is this guy's name so we can move on?"

"Lee Kershaw," I said ready to change the subject myself.

"I've actually heard of him."

"Really?"

"Yeah, mostly hearsay but I think the boys at the office have a small file on him. No arrest record and no direct links to anything illegal, but his name keeps popping up from time to time in interesting places."

"It's not going to be much help then," I said.

"Not necessarily. I'll do a little digging and see what's out there to find." My phone buzzed in my pocket making Colin roll his eyes and return to the paper. "Your new girlfriend," he mumbled.

"Not quite," I said checking the caller ID. "How are we today Madeline?" answering the phone.

"We need to talk."

"Again? I thought we did that last night."

"It will be a little different this time Jack. I'm calling with a request from my father."

I was a little surprised. "OK I guess we can work something out."

"How about a late lunch?"

"Sorry, I've got lunch plans already." I saw Colin mouth the word Alex and I shamefully nodded my head yes.

"It will have to be dinner then."

"That's fine, but tonight it will be my choice. The club was a little stuffy for this poor boy. What about Mama Santa's?"

"It's in Little Italy right?" Madeline asked.

"Yeah, can you find your way?"

"I'll manage. Can you be there at 8:00?"

At least she was asking me this time. "Sure that will be fine. See you tonight then." Colin started laughing as I hung up the phone. "What?" I asked him.

"Juggling two women. I don't know how you do it. You know if they find out they'll both kill you."

"It's not like that," I protested.

"Sure looks like it."

"Will you stop judging my social life and while you're at it, will you get off your ass and go find Kershaw for me."

Colin stared at me and then picked up the newspaper hiding his face behind it. He gave the paper a good shake that told me to go screw myself. I heard the word "asshole" mumbled from behind the sports section.

"Sorry," I said.

"That's more like it. I'll find Kershaw for you but only after I'm done with my coffee."

I looked into his cup to find it empty. "Fine," I said. "I'll leave you alone."

I got up from the table and turned to the door to leave when I heard Colin again from behind the paper. "Tell Alex I said hi." He finished off with a good laugh to himself.

Chapter 36

Meeting Madeline for dinner worked out nicely for what I had planned. It was time to find out what Chelsea knew and having Madeline talk to her would probably get the best results.

Mama Santa's Restaurant stood out like a sore thumb among the trendy trattorias dominating Cleveland's Little Italy neighborhood. It was housed in a square, red brick building, which was graced with an outdated sign and an inconspicuous pair of wooden doors. The small interior was dotted with red vinyl booths and checkered covered table cloths. Most people would say the place was in need of a remodeling job, but I loved the *Goodfellas* feel to it. The crowd at Mama Santa's was always a mix of neighborhood families and college kids who came in for a cheap dinner. Madeline would be out of her element here, but I could care less because the place was right up my alley.

The old man who greeted me at the door took me to a booth in a small room left of the main dining area. The room was darker than the rest of the place, with the walls painted an olive-green in contrast to the white walls throughout the rest of the building. I had never eaten in the room before but had often passed it on the way to the bathrooms. My imagination had always picture it as a meeting place for the heads of local families. Big and powerful Italian bosses sitting around tables with dry red wines and huge plates of homemade pasta. The room was quiet and as my fantasies flooded into my head, I noticed only two other couples around me. I would have preferred a little more noise to cover up our conversation but we could deal with it. The waitress came over after I took my seat and I ordered a plate of antipasti and a bottle of the house red while I waited for Madeline.

The antipasti came with a loaf of fresh-baked Italian bread. I grabbed a piece and immediately went for the plate of fresh, cured meats, cheeses, and a salad tossed in vinegar and oil. I thought about waiting for Madeline, but she was late and I was hungry. There was no way I could have resisted the smell of the fresh baked bread anyways, so her lateness was a good excuse to start eating.

"I know I'm a little late, but a gentleman should wait for a lady," I heard Madeline's voice say. She had come in while I was distracted, sopping up the olive oil with a piece of crust. When I looked up she smiled at me then slid into the booth.

"Sorry," I said reaching over to pour her some wine. "I was hungry but that's no excuse."

"This place is different," she said as she glanced around the room.

"Don't let appearances fool you. This is the best Italian food in Cleveland."

"Apparently," she nodded towards the half-eaten antipasti. "It looks like it once was a nice little spread."

"Once again I'm sorry." The waitress came by and we ordered a helping of veal scaloppini, a small order of the homemade ravioli, and a large pizza with the hopes that I would have some leftovers. We held off talking about business until dinner had arrived, as what seemed to be a standard practice for Madeline. Until then, we were able to keep the conversation from getting awkward with a varying array of small talk and a little dose of flirting. When the food finally arrived, I took the lead with the business talk, wanting to get out what I had to say first. "I need you to do a favor for me," I said to her.

"I'm not making any promises but what is it?"

"I need you to talk to Chelsea for me and get some details about those photos. Even if she can't remember much about the night before, or even the next morning, it still may be helpful."

Madeline sat quietly, thinking about what I had asked of her, but when she spoke, her face turned to upset. "Chelsea is not going to be of any help and if she does remember something it's a moot point now." She reached for her wine and took a long sip before pulling her purse onto her lap, taking out an envelope. "This is for you," handing it to me. "Father asked me to inform you that we are no longer in need of your services."

I was taken aback by the news and almost choked on a bite of ravioli. The Captain had seemed so dead set on protecting Chelsea, and now he was calling the whole thing off. "I'm not sure I understand."

"We have recovered the evidence being used to blackmail my sister, and that's all that matters as far as father is concerned."

"Recovered the evidence, but how? Beard was shot."

"After dinner last night, a man approached me with the photos andmemory card."

"Who was it?" I interrupted her. "He's the one who probably shot Beard."

"I can't say."

"Can't or won't?" I asked.

"I truly can't. I never saw his face."

"We still have two dead bodies. Does your father believe I can let this case go with so many unanswered questions?"

"Take a look inside the envelope, and you tell me if you will be able to let it go."

A substantial amount was inside. More than I had made in the last ten years I had worked for the government. I was being paid well to shut up and forget. "It is a nice gesture, but there is no way I can let any of this go."

"You don't get it do you Jack? There is no choice here you have to let it go. Whatever is going on is none of your business. You were hired to do a job, and the job is over. Now move on will you?"

Madeline was getting unnerved like I had never seen her before. Like every other aspect of the case, tonight was giving me more questions than answers. "Your father made it my business when he hired me," I told her firmly. "What's changed? Last night you wanted to be a detective."

"Chelsea's safety is all I ever cared about. She'll be in the clear now so please just drop it and go on with your life."

"Madeline there is more here than you are telling me. Give me something, any reason other than the money and I'll let this die. Settle my curiosity, and then I can rest."

Madeline stared at her plate toying with her veal. "I can't Jack, at least not tonight." She got up suddenly and slung her purse over her shoulder. "Please Jack back off, if only just for me," she said with watery eyes.

"I will, if you talk to Chelsea for me like I asked."

"Chelsea has done all the talking she is going to do. Goodbye Jack, and please watch yourself." Madeline turned and walked out leaving me all alone in the dark, Italian restaurant with a table full of leftovers and a mind full of questions.

Chapter 37

"Why does it have to rain all day?" Colin pondered with his head in my refrigerator. He came out with a couple of beers in hand and passed one in my direction. "Your new girlfriend still here?"

"No, Alex left after lunch today."

"Where did she run off to?"

"Sorry, I wasn't keeping track."

"You should." Colin plopped down with a heavy thud on my couch and used the remote to turn on the TV. "So she left you at dinner.?"

"We're talking about Madeline now?"

"Yeah, keep up with the conversation will you?"

"She was hiding something and I, of course, pressed the issue. Deep down Madeline had something more to say."

"Madeline is not one to talk unless she wants to. Your pressing the issue will probably just tighten those lips even more. What did she say about getting those pictures? Sounds mighty suspicious to me."

I settled into my favorite chair across from Colin and kicked my feet up on the coffee table. "Not much. Some man gave them to her after dinner and of course she never saw his face. And she was really defensive over Chelsea."

"How so?"

"I wanted her to ask Chelsea a few questions and Madeline flat out said that Chelsea had nothing to say. It was an end of the conversation statement."

"The subject of family is a sensitive one with those Gilmores," Colin said. "I'm sure they are being overprotective with Chelsea."

"Maybe, but I think there is more to it."

"You should back off and take it easy for a while. I know you won't give up on this, but maybe you could make it look like you are. You did take Captain Gilmore's money after all."

"I didn't take it. Madeline left it on the table when she took off."

"Sure she did. Either way, lay low for a day or two, at least in regards to the Gilmores. Madeline's lips might loosen up if she thinks you are doing what you're told."

"I'll think about it." I was surprised Colin wanted me to back off but he could be right about Madeline. "What did you find out about Kershaw?"

"Backing off already I see."

"Just tell me."

"OK. Kershaw is a mystery man when it comes to any documentation on him, but he is a well-known player on the street. Apparently he works for big money only and likes to play the middle man."

"What do you mean?" I asked.

"Powerful people hire Kershaw for a job, then Kershaw goes and hires it out to someone else. The person who actually does the work never knows who they are actually working for."

"A buffer between the average criminal and the powerful manipulators who don't want their hands to get dirty."

"Exactly," Colin said.

"Well it explains how Alex is involved."

"Right. I've got some more if you want it."

"I'm listening."

"Word is," Colin continued, "that Kershaw likes to have lunch at the Inn of the Barristers on East 3rd."

"Ironic place for a criminal."

"He's managed to stay clean somehow."

"I'll check it out. Any idea what he looks like? I can't be running all over town asking."

"Yeah," Colin pulled a photo from inside his suit jacket and slid it across the coffee table to me.

"Not the best shot," I said looking at the photo.

"It's all we've got."

"I'm not complaining."

"Sounded like it," Colin said before taking a sip of his beer. "What are you going to do about Madeline? Any chance you'll take my advice?"

"I'm not sure yet, but I don't want to push too hard. I could back off for a few days and let her cool, but time is of the essence with this."

"My suggestion," Colin began, "is to let her stew. Go and find Kershaw and see what he gives you. If she's ever going to come around she'll have to do it on her own."

"I hope she does because not much is making a whole lot of sense right now."

"That's the problem with you, Jack, you think everything has to make sense. Personally I never saw that in the rule book, and everyday I'm alive it gets more and more confusing."

Chapter 38

Finding Lee Kershaw was surprisingly easy. The morning after Colin gave me his photo, I trudged through the rain over to the Inn of the Barristers for lunch. A warm, corned beef sandwich, the house specialty, took the chill off, as I pretended to ignore the front door of the restaurant by watching the television behind the bar.

Finishing off the first half of my sandwich, I noticed a short man walk into the bar with a newspaper tucked under his arm and an umbrella at his side. Slightly balding, he wore a pair of thin, round frame glasses, had a well-groomed mustache, and was dressed in a tailored three-piece suit. From the photo I had stashed in my suit pocket, I knew that I was looking at Lee Kershaw. His small appearance made him look more like a banker than a criminal, but then again, was there really a difference?

Another gentleman already sitting at the bar nodded hello to Kershaw as he sat down. The bartender was there immediately with a cup of coffee and single malt Scotch. As soon as he was comfortable on the bar stool, he opened his newspaper, hiding his face from view and from anyone who might want to socialize. Within ten minutes a sandwich was placed in front of Kershaw. The usual, I assumed, a cold, corned beef sandwich with coleslaw and Swiss on rye. A good helping of Stadium Mustard was spooned onto the bread as Kershaw nibbled on the chips that came with his sandwich. He ate his food slowly while he continued to read the paper. When he was finished, he placed it on the bar, and paid for his meal in cash. He downed his untouched single malt in one gulp, and walked out.

I took my time paying my tab, not wanting to seem in a hurry, and then followed Kershaw out into the rain. Never in my wildest dreams had I planned on finding the man on the first day, so I had no plan of action. Just following him seemed appropriate at the moment. When I stepped out from the cover of the restaurant's front awning, I could barely make out Kershaw's gray suit and black umbrella through the sheets of rain. He was heading south on East 3rd towards Public Square at a leisurely pace. I found his casual pace surprising with the rain coming down as hard as it was. If I had been going anywhere farther than three blocks it would have been in a dry cab.

Kershaw walked all the way to Tower City Center where he cut through to the downtown mall. The place was dry which was good, but the mall was nearly empty, making it impossible to follow him without being seen. Kershaw was not bothering to do any window shopping as he walked straight through the mall then out through the Huron Road exit. He crossed the street, barely pausing for the busy traffic that I decided to safely wait for. While I waited for a city bus to pass, I had a good view of where Kershaw was heading and watched as he walked through the sliding glass doors of the Rock 'n' Roll Casino. By the time I was able to catch up, and make my way inside, Kershaw had disappeared somewhere on the casino floor. I stood for a moment, hoping to catch a glimpse of him, but all I was left with were the sounds of slot machines and a pair of cold, wet shoes.

Chapter 39

"I'm being followed," Kershaw said as he sat in one of the black leather chairs Daniel Shaw had in his office.

"Is that what you came here to tell me?"

"No, I just noticed it on the way over here from lunch."

"Try breaking up your routine once in a while and it might be a little harder to follow you."

Kershaw really hated Daniel Shaw. Every ounce of him became frustrated simply at the thought of the man. "Why should I change my routine? You eat at Morton's every day."

"But who is the one being followed? Why are we even talking about this? I hope you were smart enough to lose the tail. Now, why are you really here?"

Shaw seemed really at ease today, almost happy, and it had Kershaw a little worried. "It's about the money you owe me."

"What about it?"

"I haven't received the funds you promised me."

"Ah yes, about that. I have decided to hold onto the money until you have completed your job for me. All of your screw ups recently have gotten me thinking that I need to see these tasks followed through until they are finished up completely."

"I get paid before the job. You know how it works Shaw," Kershaw was yelling now. "I want my money now or I will let everything unravel on you!"

"No threats Lee. You don't have the means to back them up. Besides, the way I see it you can't afford to let things unravel. You are being followed remember."

"I want my money. This is not how we do business. You pay me and then I do the job you pay me to do. That's how it works."

"That's how it used to work and maybe in the future it can again, but only after you regain my confidence." The whole time Shaw remained calm, which was very uncharacteristic of him. "In fact, if you're not content with this arrangement, I will have to find someone else to work with in the future. Lee, let me point out the obvious to you. If you are being followed, then you must be a person of interest to somebody. Now I would suggest you go and clean up the mess you've made before you find yourself in jail or dead." There was a definite threat to the last part.

"I really think all this," Kershaw looked around the office, "is going to your head. Do you seriously believe that if they can pin anything on me then they won't find a way to get you too? You're not as untouchable as you may think Shaw."

"All this, as you say, has gone to my head and I love it. As for my involvement in any activities, you are the only one who knows about them. So how exactly will anyone find out if you are dead?"

"I thought you said no threats."

"Unlike you, Lee, I have the means to back them up."

Kershaw was stuck and he hated himself for it, but he hated Daniel Shaw even more. He wanted to shoot the man dead right where he sat behind his big, rich desk. Shaw had placed himself in a powerful position and Kershaw had no leverage to work with. He got up from his chair and grabbed his umbrella.

"Oh Lee," Shaw said.

"What?"

"The man following you, I would suspect it is Jack Francis."

"Yeah that's what I figured, but how did you know?"

"I keep myself informed. Now you may want to do something to get him off your back. I would start by leaving through the garage entrance."

"Why is that," Kershaw asked.

Shaw pointed to a bank of screens behind Kershaw. One of them was zoomed in on Jack Francis playing a slot machine. "Be careful Lee. He seems to be a persistent man."

Chapter 40

The past few nights had consisted of little sleep so as I went to bed, I was looking forward to a long peaceful rest. However, nothing ever works out like you plan, and to my dismay, the phone woke me up around two the next morning. I noticed the rain still doing its dance along my window as I answered the phone with an unpleasant tone. "What?"

"I've got something you might want to see," I heard Colin's voice on the other end.

"It better be good you woke me up."

"Just trying to repay the favor from the other night."

"We're even now," I grumbled.

"Sure, now wake up and put some clothes on."

"I don't wanna," I whined into the phone like a baby. "It better be good if I'm going to go out in the rain."

"I already told you it was. Now head over to the west bank of the Flats and meet me by the Norfolk and Southern Railroad Bridge. You won't be able to miss me."

"Alright, I'm on my way," I moaned, hanging up the phone and reaching for a pair of pants on the chair next to my bed.

It took me five minutes to get ready and most of the time was used up waiting for a pot of coffee to brew. I threw on an old rain coat and with coffee in hand I went down to the street to meet the cab I had called. The cab driver seemed as unhappy as I was to be out in the rain at such an hour, but who could blame him. He never even blinked when I told him to drive me to a railroad bridge in the Flats. I would have found it odd considering the once thriving party district was now nothing more than a ghost town. Maybe he already knew something I didn't.

By the time the cab crossed the Cuyahoga River and was winding its way down into the Flats, there was no doubt as to where I was going. Most of the river bank shimmered from the spotlights and flashing colors from emergency vehicles. The lights were ricocheting off of the wet roads and old warehouse windows, creating quite a spectacle. The cabby did his best to make his way as close as possible but was ultimately stopped by a Cleveland Police road block. They had cordoned off a large area keeping out any unwanted reporters. Journalist would flock like vultures anytime this many flashing lights came together.

I paid the driver, got out of the cab, and was back in the rain where I started looking for Colin. I pulled my coat tighter around me trying to stay dry, while I waited outside the barricade for a young black and white to go find Colin for me. The kid was fast and within minutes Colin was whisking me through the ranks of public servants.

"This better be good," I mumbled to him as we made our way to the river bank.

"Oh it is." Colin pointed through the rain towards the river where I could make out a car being pulled from the water. It was a silver Mercedes.

"Is that Madeline's?" I asked apprehensively.

"Nope, it belongs to Chelsea."

Chapter 41

"A diver called it in," Colin said, as the car sat on the gravel bank. Brown, river water drained from the vehicle and mixed in with puddles of rain. "They were welding some of the supports for the bridge below the waterline. C.P.D. got the call."

"What took them so long to pull it out?" I asked.

"They had trouble getting a salvage crew out here, and with all the rain it wasn't an easy job to begin with."

The techies were now beginning to gather around the car anxious to give it the once over. "How did you end up here so quickly?"

"A buddy of mine with C.P.D. took the call, and after they confirmed the plates he called me. Apparently the car has been missing since Chelsea's little night in Bratenahl." Even through the rain Colin must have been able to read the expression on my face. "I'm guessing Captain Gilmore forgot to tell you."

"Must have slipped his mind."

"It seems Chelsea told him she left it in the Warehouse District where she was out at a club. The old man filed a report the next day when they couldn't find it parked anywhere. He had Douglas call it in."

"Is it possible the Captain wasn't able to make the connection between the missing car and the blackmailer?"

"He might be getting old," Colin said, "but his mind is still good. If he didn't tell you about the car then he did it on purpose."

We stared in silence and watched a couple of local detectives try to pry the trunk open. The electronics had been fried by the river water causing a slight problem when trying to pop the trunk. After a few minutes one of the salvage crew walked over with a crowbar and motioned to the two detectives to step aside. Like an old pro, the trunk popped open on the first try. "We've got a body!" A grizzled voice yelled from the crowd huddled around the car. It was like a call to the pigs at feeding time as everyone on site rushed to get a look. Nothing seems to attract human interest faster than a little death.

Colin and I pushed our way through the rest of onlookers, which was comprised of mostly black and whites who rarely get to see a body. Finally, it was the two of us and a couple of forensic guys staring into the trunk. To my relief the body belonged to a man. The fire prone waters of the Cuyahoga had not been much help in preserving him. The man's skin appeared soggy as if it would slide right off of the bone, and where it was mostly a pale color, it was also somehow purple at the same time. His eyes were lifeless and rolled back into his head and his hands were shriveled up like prunes. Matted, botchy hair nearly covered the entry wound at the back of the skull, and when I noticed the clothes on the body, I knew we had found the missing victim from Chelsea's photos.

"It's the body from the pictures," I mumble to Colin so no one else could hear. "Same entry point and same clothes."

"I'll get you an official I.D. on it as soon as I can but to save you some time, I'm pretty sure I know who it is."

"Levi Zeitlin?" I asked.

"That's my guess. Even in such bad shape it looks like him."

"Unfortunately for Levi, I now have a strong lead to follow. Find a motive for killing him and I guarantee I can figure out this whole mess I've found myself in."

"Good luck with that," Colin scoffed.

"What, you don't want to help?"

"You'll have the full help of my expertise, unofficially of course."

"Of course."

Chapter 42

The man looked through the unattached scope of a sniper rifle at the scene below him on the river bank. He was perched in an abandoned warehouse on a hill above the flood plain. He dropped the scope from his eye and began to smile to himself. The flashing lights below bounced across the shadows of the building and reflected off his dark eyes, a piercing black. The body was to have never been found, at least that was how his employer wanted it, but he was tired of Cleveland and now he had his own motives. What he wanted always took precedent and he was not afraid of repercussions from Lee Kershaw, old man Gilmore, or anyone else for that matter. Nobody had any idea who he really was or even a hint of what he was capable of. Well, they did have a small taste and it was probably enough to keep them from ever trying to hunt him down. Tonight though was about one thing and one person. It was time to fry the big fish.

He pulled a cell phone from his pocket. The man grinned as he remembered taking it from the lifeless body of Levi Zeitlin. When he began to dial the phone the irony only gave him more confidence.

"Hello," Daniel Shaw answered.

"Good evening Mr. Shaw." The raspy voice with the hint of a European accent was gone. Tonight the man spoke like an average American, Midwest accent and all.

"Who is this?"

"I'm an employee of yours Mr. Shaw."

"I'm sorry it's a little late to be speaking with employees and especially on my private line. How did you get this number?" Shaw's voice was demanding and authoritative, but deep down inside the man reeked of concern.

"How did you like my coffee mug, Mr. Shaw?"

"The what," Daniel Shaw paused when realization hit him. "You, I will kill you if I ever get my hands on you. Nobody threatens me you slimy little bastard."

"Now, now Daniel," the man scolding him like a child, "we need not lose our temper. We need to stay nice and calm so we can have an adult conversation."

"Go screw yourself. Who the hell are you anyway?"

"Calm yourself and maybe we can talk a little business. Maybe even answer a few of those questions I know you have." The man was as cool as always and was finding real enjoyment in Daniel Shaw's outbursts.

"There will be no business. Not with you or anyone else who threatens me."

"Fine if that's the way you want it. Oh, before I go you might want to know that the local cops with the help of a few Feds are currently pulling Levi Zeitlin's body from the trunk of Chelsea Gilmore's Mercedes."

"That's not possible," Shaw said in disbelief.

"It's quite possible. Look out your office window Daniel," intentionally using his first name to establish who was in charge. "I'm sure you'll be able to see the lights down the river from where your office is."

There was a long silence as Shaw looked north out of his office window catching the reflection of police lights along the river. "You are still getting nothing out of me. I told you I do not deal with threats."

"That's fine with me, Daniel. You can go right ahead and play the tough guy if you want, but when those nice detectives start looking for a motive your name will eventually come up. Think about it and I'll be in touch. Oh, Daniel one last thing..."

"Screw you."

"Not very nice, Daniel. Its time you learned that you're not as untouchable as you might think." The man hung up the phone and tossed it out of the warehouse window. It fell four stories down onto the pavement with a shatter. He put the scope back up to his eye and watched his handy work below. There among the crowd he noticed Jack Francis nosing around where he didn't belong.

Chapter 43

Lee Kershaw had nearly lost his appetite as he put his phone down on the bar inside the Inn of the Barristers. Daniel Shaw had been throwing down orders from the heavens with all the ego of a man fueled by power and anger. A smile crossed Kershaw's face as he thought about where such continued behavior would lead Shaw. If Shaw was a man in a normal position then he would have been destined to get his, but it wasn't that simple with someone as high up in the pecking order as he was. However, even though the phone call from Shaw was ruining his mood, the half-eaten sandwich in front of him was calling him. Business could wait, he thought, as he picked up his paper and continued his lunch. At least there was no one here to follow him today.

The rain had changed into a misting as it slowly began to taper off. The past few days had brought spring like weather into the city but it wouldn't last. September was only a few days away and there was still plenty of time for more heat, Kershaw thought, as he stepped outside to leave the bar. He pulled his phone out the moment he hit the sidewalk preparing to do Daniel Shaw's bidding. Kershaw knew it was well past time to find a new source of income.

"What is it now," the raspy voice answered. Kershaw thought it may have sounded a little Czech.

"I've got something for you."

"How interesting," the man's voice came out snake like.

"Jimmy DeLuca..."

"Yes, I know you have already requested that one."

"And someone else too."

"I was waiting for this one. Let me guess the woman is it? Alex, I believe is her name."

Kershaw was a little surprised by the man's correct answer, but then again he had all kinds of tricks up his sleeve. "Yes, Alex too," Kershaw said paining at the words leaving his lips.

"It would appear as if someone has suddenly decided to do some house cleaning. You do realize with these two taken care of, all that is left is you Kershaw?"

There was silence across the phone for a moment as the weight of the man's words settled around Kershaw. "And you as well," he finally was able to reply.

"Oh, I'm not sure I really count seeing that I only exist to you. Besides I wouldn't worry yourself. You are Daniel Shaw's go to guy. I am sure he will want to keep you around."

"Who said anything about Daniel Shaw?"

"Only trying to strike up some conversation," the man laughed as he pictured Kershaw squirming on the other end of the phone. "I prefer my clients to think things through first. Have you Kershaw? Have you really thought this through all of the way?"

"I am aware of what needs to be done," but Kershaw was now a little unsure. Things were beginning to spiral and pile up all at the same time, and he would love to deflect some of it in another direction.

"Alright, if that is all, I will take care of Alex and Jimmy for you."

"One more thing," Kershaw spurted out quickly before he was hung up on.

"It's already becoming a very expensive tab you're running."

"You'll get yours," Kershaw answered.

"I always do." The man's voice was cold and threatening, leaving Kershaw with a stark reality of who he was dealing with.

"I need you to get Jack Francis off of my back," Kershaw told the man.

"And how am I supposed to know who that is?"

"You know who I'm talking about, or at least you are fully capable of finding out. I don't need you playing games with me on this one."

"Very well, I was only trying to give you a hard time," laughing at how tight Kershaw's nerves were, he continued, "By getting him off your back do you mean to add him to the list with Alex and young Jimmy?"

"Not yet, there is too much of that going on already. See what you can do by other means."

"I am most certain that Mr. Francis can be handled." The man knew that Jack Francis was now following the Zeitlin lead he had left in the river. It would have him out of Kershaw's hair for a little while. "Kershaw," the man said.

"What?"

"Watch yourself. A man like Daniel Shaw is likely to be very unstable," and with one last rotten laugh, the call ended.

Chapter 44

Layered somewhere between the dead bodies and the blackmail was one simple fact that continued to slap me across the face. Almost no one involved was being straight with me and it was making my job a lot harder to do. The whole Gilmore family, whom at first seemed to be the victims, now appeared as problematic as the criminals they accused. In fact, only out of the criminal element was I was beginning to find a reliable person— Alex, who was slowly building up some trust with me. Colin was the most reliable person involved, which went without saying. For years he had been my most trusted friend and even with his wife Katya's connections to Captain Gilmore, there was no doubt as to where he stood. He was my best resource for accurate information but it could be severely limited due to his position with the Bureau.

Whether or not I could trust someone didn't determine their usefulness to me. Each person was different and if I knew where they stood, then I could determine what was truth and what was a blatant lie. Sometimes identifying the lies could tell you more than the truth. Getting information out of someone depended on the proper use of the right techniques. Since Alex now held middle ground with me, she would be the first person I went after, the Gilmores second, and I would leave Colin to his own devices. His information would come willingly but only when he could give it to me.

The day after Levi Zeitlin's body was found in the back of Chelsea Gilmore's car, the rain finally began to taper off. The air was cool and damp, almost misty, and I took it as a precursor to a cold winter to come. With any luck I would escape Cleveland's snowy weather for a warmer climate before it buried me in. For now, I stood looking out of my condo window at a miserable day at the end of August. I still had a few months to get out of town before the cold came down across the lake from Canada. I turned from the window and focused my thoughts to Alex, sitting on the sofa sipping some Earl Grey.

"I told you already Jack I cannot help you with any of this," Alex said, breaking to take a sip of her tea. "Not unless I want to end up on the bottom of the river too."

"I'm not asking you do to anything involved with your work."

"How so?"

"Because I am not asking about you, Kershaw, or anyone else you might be involved with. I just want to know about the Zeitlin kid. I need some information on him so I can try to figure out a motive."

"I'm sure your FBI pal has the resources for that," Alex said.

"For some of it, sure, but not for what I want." I moved to the chair and sat looking at Alex face to face. "Now don't take this the wrong way, but I need to know if he was involved in something a little seedier, something that someone in your position might hear about as a rumor."

"Talk about something illegal, is that what you're asking? Find out if the kid stuck his nose in someone else's business.?"

"Sorry, I wasn't insinuating anything." I had noticed a change in her tone but she waved her hand as if to say no apology was needed. "I'm just trying to use all the resources available to me that's all. I didn't mean anything by it."

Alex got up from the sofa and went into the kitchen where I heard the water begin to run as she rinsed out her tea cup. She spoke as she came back into the living room. "I'll see what I can do but if I find something out it doesn't mean I have to tell you."

"Why not?"

She came over and sat on my lap with her arms around my neck and her face close to mine. "Jack why did you have to make this complicated. We could have been great friends with benefits but now you want me to be your sidekick and I just can't do that. I'll give you anything I find, but I will not jeopardize my life for you. I think we both know where all of your digging will lead and we know that the chances are I won't be able to follow you there without finding myself in trouble."

"Are we still talking about the case or us?" I asked sincerely.

"Does it matter?"

"Yes, because I'm getting confused."

"Well then let me simplify it for you. No matter what my feelings are for you Jack, I won't allow them to make me do something stupid."

"I would never ask you to do more than what is right."

"Your definition of what is right and mine probably differ some."

"Alex you'll know what to do if, and when, you find yourself in a position to help."

"Come here," Alex said kissing me and ruffling my hair. "Sometimes you are so naïve." All I could do was smile and stare into her big eyes hoping I had judged the woman correctly.

Chapter 45

After several failed attempts at trying to hunt down Chelsea, I decided to go for another approach. I had staked out the house and a couple of her favorite bars with no luck. Either the young woman was locked in the house or out of the city. Captain Gilmore was the next person I wanted a word with, but each time I tried, his assistant Douglas blocked me and reminded me of my unemployed status with the old man. Douglas was polite enough until I pressed a little too far and he cut off contact with me as well. The only person out of the Gilmores willing to speak to me was Madeline, but even that had been hard to negotiate. It was only after an extensive amount of badgering on my part did she finally decide to give me a bone to chew on.

Madeline had been willing to meet me at the Greenhouse Tavern where Katya worked behind the bar. I was hoping Katya's presence would help to put pressure on Madeline to tell me the truth. I also figured Katya would be able to read Madeline a little bit better than I could, having known her longer.

"I still don't know why you want to bring that woman in here," Katya said placing my bourbon in front of me. I sat gnawing on a plate of gravy frites trying to avoid her glare. "I have no interest in seeing her."

"I am hoping she feels the same about you. It would be nice to have her distracted or at least get her emotions running so she might slip up."

"Good luck, lying comes second nature in that family."

Within seconds of Katya's comments, the door opened and like a whirlwind Madeline entered pulling off her jacket and purse in one motion. She tossed them onto the stool next to her as she swiftly sat down. "How are we today, Katya?" she asked using the royal "we."

"I'm good Maddie. I know it's never too early for you to drink, so what will it be?" Katya fired back with vile.

"Glad to see you are still playing the role of good little servant." I almost choked on Madeline's comment as I stuffed a pile of gravy and mozzarella covered frites in my mouth. "I'll have bourbon. Whatever Jack is drinking will do."

Shit, I thought, *don't pull me into this*. It was too late though Madeline had already set her eyes on me. "Glad to see you are in a good mood today Madeline," I said finally swallowing my food. Katya set a bourbon on the rocks down in front of Madeline and walked to the other end of the bar. She stood with arms crossed and eyes glaring death right in our direction. "Are we in the mood to talk today?" I asked Madeline throwing the royal "we" back at her.

"It depends. Chelsea is off limits."

"Why are you protecting her? I'm not out to hurt your sister."

"She's my sister and I'm looking out for her. Besides she's not around to talk to you but I am here, so what is it you want from me?"

"She's not around," I was surprised by her direct use of those words. "Where is she?"

"Chelsea is off limits period. Now I'm here so talk to me." Madeline's jaw hardened with stubbornness.

"Alright," I relented. "Tell me what you know about Levi Zeitlin."

"Friends with my sister, parents dead and left every penny to him, and now he runs around like a little playboy," she listed.

"Is that it?"

"Pretty much, why?"

"Well," I paused a moment, "his body was pulled from the Cuyahoga River last night."

"My God that is terrible, but I never hung out with him like Chelsea did."

I found it funny that when a dead body was back in the discussion, Chelsea's name resurfaced. Madeline didn't want to talk about her sister, but the topic was becoming impossible to avoid.

"Why are you telling me all of this?" Madeline asked.

I wondered if she knew what was coming next.

"I really wanted to have this conversation with your sister, but since you and your father will not allow it, you are the next best thing." Madeline looked as if she wanted to speak but I kept moving so she would not have a chance. "There is something else you should know before you say anything more. His body was found in the trunk of Chelsea's missing car. The one nobody bothered to tell me was missing."

Madeline played shocked very well. "How," came out first and then, "Why weren't we called and told the car was found?"

"Your father is probably getting the call right now." Colin had pulled some strings to have the call held off for awhile so I could get a chance to talk to Madeline. She seemed almost angry at what was happening but she was only able to show very little emotion. Instead she looked away and reached for her cell phone in her purse. As she stood I fired one last comment , "If you are calling your father tell him I said hi, and if you are calling

Chelsea then ask her why someone would want to kill Levi." Madeline gave me a long hard look then turned towards the ladies room.

Katya came back over the moment Madeline had gone to the restroom. "She looked genuinely surprised."

"But was it because of the news or because Madeline realized she had been played. Let's hope it was the news and maybe it will help draw something out of her."

Chapter 46

When Madeline returned from the restroom the cell phone had been put away and she had regained her strong composure. Rigid, firm, and confident, she walked back to her bar stool and stared Katya down as Katya retreated from us once more.

"Have the two of you been conspiring in my absence?" Madeline nodded towards Katya now at the end of the bar speaking with another customer.

"Friendly chat that's all. Is the family all up to date?

"It seems you had this all planned out." Madeline did not appear amused with that reality.

"I don't follow." I said in attempt to feign innocence.

"Colin was the one to call father about the car. It seems a little odd that it was him and not the local police."

"Isn't he friends with the family? Maybe it was a courtesy to your old man."

"You can call it what you want but I think he held off the news until you had gotten your chance to talk to me."

Smart girl, I thought. "Maybe, but what does it matter."

"It matters because I need to be able to trust you Jack."

"What, like I can trust you? Have you been the least bit honest during this whole escapade with your sister?"

"I have never lied to you."

I laughed with no remorse for the woman. "I'm not sure if that's true, but what I do know is you are a professional at pushing the boundaries of the truth."

"Withholding information is not lying."

"Not much different than lying, in my book."

"You are welcome to your opinion." Madeline seemed a little frustrated and the easy loss of composure made me realize something big must be bothering her. When I first met her she was a rock, never flinching. Now she anxiously played with the glass in front of her, twirling it between her hands.

"I don't want to sit here and debate ethics with you. What I want is anything you have withheld from me. Anything at all I might be able to use in finding Levi Zeitlin's killer."

"Why do you even care? My father paid you well, so why not just forget about Levi and let the local police do their job?"

"Your father gave me a job to finish. For some reason your family believes that it's done, but I do not. There is more here, and when I take something on I like to follow it through to the end."

"What is it Jack, something with your moral conscious?"

"Seems like it."

"Believe it or not, you are a very selfish person." Madeline's eyes were tired and I hoped she was breaking down from all the banter. Making a person really think about a situation usually helped them open up to the right road.

"Moral to a fault then I guess." I smiled at her hoping to warm her up a little more. It appeared my morality was something I could occasionally use to my advantage, and today was one of those times.

"Its Colin's fault I guess." Madeline glanced down the bar towards Katya. "He recommended you to my father. I bet he even knew how you would respond. I bet he knew all about your never give up attitude. It's just like Colin to do something like that since he's a save the day cowboy too."

I laughed again, not trying to ease the mood, but because she was right. Well, the cowboy thing was way off but she nailed the rest right on the head. "Madeline, why not help me then if you know I won't quit?"

"Because my family comes first."

"You are as stubborn as your old man. None of you give a shit about Levi's death at all. Only thing you care about is protecting your precious Gilmore name."

"Levi Zeitlin was a waste of a life to start with. It is probably better off he is dead because now his inheritance will go to charity and not up his nose. You know Jack, if he was still alive he would have probably overdosed eventually, or killed someone else driving intoxicated all over this town." Madeline was really fired up and any remorse toward Levi was definitely not there.

"Wow, Madeline, why so cold?"

"It is simply the truth. Just because someone is dead doesn't mean I have to change my opinion of them." She stood up and put her coat on. Her purse was pulled over her shoulder with the force of a defiant teenager. "Jack, I don't know why Levi was killed or why Chelsea had to be blackmailed. The reality of it is Chelsea's blackmailer is gone and she is off the hook."

"Convenient," I quickly interjected.

She rolled her eyes at me and continued on her little speech. "I'm sorry Levi is dead but it is still no concern of mine. For all I know it had to do with his drug habit, his gambling habit, or his little mistress. There are too many reasons someone could want a kid like Levi killed."

"Who is his mistress?" I had never heard of her before and was already thinking about the possibility of another lead.

"I have no idea. Chelsea seemed to think he had one."

"So you did talk to Chelsea again?"

"Not important."

"It might be."

"Drop it Jack. Chelsea just mentioned that Levi was prone to running off sometimes with a married woman. It was always a spur of the moment thing. She had no idea who and neither do I." She turned toward the door and began to leave.

"Madeline."

"That's all I've got for you Jack."

"Madeline," I called again.

"What?" Finally turning back to look at me.

"Thanks." No response other than a cold shoulder as she walked out of the bar.

Katya came back down to my end of the bar almost immediately. "I told you she was trouble. The woman is simply frustrating."

"Stubborn too," I added.

"She's hiding something from you," Katya said.

"Probably, but she appeared to be truthful about Levi."

"Makes me really want to know what she's hiding then."

"I'm not sure I really want to know," thinking about where the possibilities might lead.

Chapter 47

There was no reason to trust Lee Kershaw and no reason to want to, but Alex had questions that only he could answer. The late summer sun had finally returned to Cleveland with a vengeance and Alex sat soaking up every bit of it at a café table on East 4th. Wearing a low-cut sun dress, she had put her hair up in a ponytail and donned a pair of tortoise shell Wayfarers. She liked looking her best when meeting with Kershaw, because he was known to become distracted by a woman's assets. It was the only way she knew to get through some of his defenses.

Everywhere around her the street was brimming full of people sharing the nice weather and the last days of summer. There was one who stood out and completely out of place.

"Jesus Lee," Alex said, "lose the suit it's over ninety and you look like you're sweating to death.

Haven't you noticed everyone around you is dressed for summer?"

"It was a fine thing to wear until you made me come outside." Kershaw sat in the chair across the table from her, and dabbed sweat from his forehead with a handkerchief he pulled out of his pants pocket. "Why not pick a table inside and do me a favor for once?"

"I'm working on my tan. In a few months I'll have to pay for one, and besides I was smart enough to dress for the weather."

"I can see that," Kershaw said as he sloppily looked her over.

"Stop staring at my tits, Lee. Why does every conversation we have start with me telling you that."

"Alright," he said as he gained his composure a little. "So what is you want from me anyway?"

"I wanted to report in."

"What?"

"I am still working a job for you or am I wrong?"

Kershaw seemed flustered by the thought, almost as if he had forgotten about the job he had sent Alex on only days ago. "No, you're right. I've just been busy. What is it you've got for me?"

"Nothing," Alex said. "It appears the Gilmores have recovered the antique dealer's blackmail evidence though."

"Did you let Jack Francis beat you to it?"

"Not quite. Apparently the photos were recovered by another unknown party. I can guarantee that it's not Mr. Francis. I also know Mr. Francis is equally clueless as to who it is."

"Are you sure?" asked Kershaw.

"I'm sure," Alex said with a mischievous smile.

"Do I need to ask how?"

"Don't bother Lee. Anyways, the Gilmores are in possession of the photos, so where does that leave us?"

"Stuck I guess. I don't know if Mr. Shaw is going to be pleased with this news, but with the Gilmores holding onto those pictures of Chelsea, we can be certain they'll never get out."

"So it was Daniel Shaw this whole time." Alex had assumed as much, but she never dreamed the words would come from Kershaw's lips.

"Not like you didn't already know." Kershaw was still perspiring through his suit as he sat uneasy in his chair.

"Lee, are you ok? It's a bit odd of you to volunteer such information even though we all knew who was giving the orders."

"I'm fine, the heat is all. Do you need anything else from me, Alex? If not, I'm going to go and find some air conditioning."

"Since you are so open with your secrets today, why not let me in on another one?"

"Ask, but I'll probably lie to you."

"I always assume that Lee. Why not tell me why Shaw wanted the kid dead in the first place?"

"I'm not sweating enough to tell you that. Besides, I have no idea. He pays me for a job and I get it done. No questions asked."

"Sure Lee, whatever you say. We both know that you have a pretty good idea even if Daniel Shaw didn't come right out and tell you."

"I sure do." Kershaw patted down his forehead once again as he stood up from the table. "Alex, let me tell you this, and I'm only saying it because it won't matter much longer. Daniel Shaw can screw anyone in this city and get away with it, but no one can screw Daniel Shaw. Unfortunately most people learn it the hard way."

"Lee," Alex said as the man began to walk away. "Thanks for your help."

"I don't deserve it," was all she heard him mumble as he disappeared into the crowded street.

Chapter 48

He didn't know what bothered him more, the guilt about ordering the hit on Alex, or the fact that he had allowed himself to care about her life. She was pleasant enough and great to look at, but what was really eating at him about the whole situation was Daniel Shaw, sitting in his river view office getting away scot-free while he agonized over the whole mess. Kershaw knew from the moment Jimmy DeLuca screwed up that he was probably going to end up a dead man, but Alex was a different situation. She was brought in to help clean up someone else's mess and had done her job like she had been told. Too bad she had to die simply because Shaw was getting nervous. The more Kershaw thought about it the more he began to fear for his own life. His only hope was that Shaw's nerves would calm down once Alex and Jimmy were out of the picture.

Walking into a little sushi place in the Warehouse District, Kershaw ordered a cucumber roll, an ice water, and some cold sake. It was too early for the dinner crowd and a little late in the afternoon for lunch so the place was quiet, except for Kershaw's thoughts. He sat thinking about what his next move should be, as the man behind the counter rolled Asian pear, avocado, and salmon into a thin sheet of cucumber before topping it with ponzu. Calling Daniel Shaw about the Gilmore's retrieving the pictures, was what he should do, but he wasn't very optimistic about the man's reaction, especially since he had originally told him they had been destroyed. There was a chance Shaw would be relieved about the evidence of the Zeitlin kid's murder being off the street. The more likely scenario ended with Shaw screaming through the phone about Kershaw letting the pictures slip through his fingers. The call could wait.

He suddenly had another thought, which basically told old Daniel Shaw to go screw himself. The more Kershaw dwelled on it, the happier he was with himself. Why did Shaw even need to know about the pictures? Right now they were considered destroyed, and for all Kershaw cared, he could go right on believing that. Sure Shaw would be pissed if they ever showed up again, but not nearly as mad as he would be now if he knew someone else had their hands on them. Nothing made Daniel Shaw angrier then someone else having something he wanted. The reason it would work is because he knew old Captain Gilmore would never let those pictures of Chelsea out of his sight. Most likely, they had already been destroyed.

The sushi began to taste even better as he decided that doing nothing was going to be his best policy. He would sit quiet, keep a low profile, and avoid Shaw until the whole mess had blown over. Jimmy and Alex would still have to die, but Kershaw's newfound guilt over Alex had already begun to disappear with every sip of his sake. Over time, Daniel Shaw would be distracted with other matters, and the murder of Levi Zeitlin would become an afterthought. Kershaw took another long drink of the cold sake and as it slid down his throat all his troubles and the hot summer's day slowly began to disappear. His nerves were settling and his mind was at ease. If he only knew his tranquility would be short-lived, he would have never left the sushi bar.

Chapter 49

The body was bruised, bloodied, and writhing in pain, in an abandoned steel yard south of the city. The man stood above watching with carnal pleasure at the agony he was inflicting on the near corpse sputtering on the ground. He slowly circled the body to reveal the barely recognizable face of Jimmy DeLuca. The man smiled at what life remained in Jimmy's eyes before he laid a steel toe right into his nose and reveled in the spray of blood it created.

The man bent down close enough to whisper into Jimmy's ear. "It never pays to be sloppy kid," his raspy voice lectured. It was his absolute favorite voice to use. A psychological advantage over his potential prey and victims, the voice foreshadowed the evil he was capable of creating. The raspy, soft tone reflected how he worked his victims with cool composure and a deadly strike. Poor Jimmy DeLuca had been blind to his attack. The kid never suspected a country bumpkin with a Midwestern accent. The fool, the man thought as he looked at the young man too helpless to save his own life.

A stolen beat up truck was parked on the gravel behind them. The man always played his parts well and the truck was a great prop for his country boy routine. From the back of the truck he retrieved an ax and a long length of rope. Jimmy's fear was boiling out into the air, and as he breathed, it filled him with the excitement and anticipation of the kill. Often his kills had to be swift and clean, but when he was allowed time to work and perform, his art became priceless. The rope was tied around Jimmy's wrists and his arms were stretched out. The length of rope was then thrown over one of the beams in the roof of the old steel mill, and for a moment Jimmy thought he was about to be hung. "That would be too easy," the man said reading the kid's mind. The man began to show his teeth as his smile grew. The man was amused at the lack of imagination from the kid. What was planned for Jimmy DeLuca would be a lot more fun than a little lynching.

Picking up the ax, the man stood above Jimmy who was still on the ground unable to move. He looked down on the helpless soul like a God with the power to give life or take it away. Today, this God would take Jimmy's life and thrive from the pleasure. The ax swung down towards Jimmy quickly and without warning. The smooth, powerful swing took Jimmy's left foot, and before his screams could reach the air, the second stroke removed his right foot, and blood poured out onto the ground.

Moving with focused determination, the man pulled hard on the rope hanging from the beam above him. Jimmy was lifted by his tied wrists into the air where his battered body swung and bled beneath the roof of the old steel mill. The young man's severed feet lay on the ground below him as his life and blood sprayed out of his body, flicking across the ground like paint on an artist's canvas. To the man holding the ax, it was a work of art. Jimmy had gone from prey to hunted game, strung up and drained of his life, finally transformed into the work of a master.

The man waited and watched until the very end not wanting to miss a moment. When the soul of Jimmy DeLuca departed, so did the man who had taken his life, leaving behind the kid's body and the gun that was used to shoot Levi Zeitlin. Pulling out of the river valley and the steelyards, he thought about how much he enjoyed driving the old pickup truck and even contemplated getting one when he left the city for good. Jimmy DeLuca was already a forgotten memory.

Chapter 50

The lead on the Zeitlin boy was getting me no where, and I had been unable to dig up anything on his rumored mistress. Alex had been of little help, only confirming what I already knew but volunteering nothing new to my investigation. She seemed preoccupied of late and I had chosen not to press the issue any further with her.

I did manage to convince Colin it was a good idea to track down Levi Zeitlin's phone records even though it was an obvious breach of Cleveland police jurisdiction. The FBI had ways of getting around the rules and Colin knew most of them. A cell phone was never found on Levi's body when it was recovered from the trunk of Chelsea's car, but who was living today without one? The odds were pretty good the rich socialite had a cell phone, a V.I.P. call list, and hopefully somewhere in it, the number of his most recent illicit hookup.

The summer heat had returned with full force and I wandered the city streets with nothing better to do than think. I was at an impasse in the investigation and seemed stuck in a position where I was reliant on others to move forward. It was a hard position for me to deal with because it made me feel like my skills were lacking and I was in need of a little life support to keep my case going. I walked slowly down the concrete sidewalks in a pair of seersucker shorts, a white shirt, and a cozy pair of flip-flops before finally stopping in a patio bar on East 4th. I ordered a cold Corona and felt the bottle sweat from my palm and down the length of my arm. The beer was transporting my mind to a beach where the trade winds blew, when I noticed two people sitting at a table just down the street from me. One had the look of a 1950s Hollywood star and the other was sweating to death in a suit. Alex and Kershaw were having a little meeting. What were they up to?

I watched the two of them for a few minutes looking for their body language to tell me about the conversation, since I could not hear from my vantage point. Kershaw, looking like a man on the verge of a heart attack, finally stood and walked down the street. Nothing said the conversation ended badly, but there was no reason to believe the opposite either. Alex sat well collected and asked the waitress for the check before leaving the table for the crowded street. My first instinct was to follow her, but with the amount of people on the street she would be lost before I could even ask the bartender for my tab. I was seriously thinking about skipping out on the bill and coming back later to settle up when my cell vibrated from the pocket of my shorts.

"Make it quick, I'm a little busy," I answered.

"Not for this you're not," Colin said.

"Alex and Kershaw just had a little meet and greet. Do you have something better than that?"

"Told you the woman was trouble, and yes I do have something better."

"Well, are you going to tell me or just leave me hanging," I asked realizing I wasn't sure if I really wanted the answer.

"Let's put it this way," Colin said, "I think the local boys are going to solve the Levi Zeitlin murder for you."

"There is no way I'm going to believe that. You'll have to give me a little more to go on."

"Patience Jack, besides it will be better if I fill you in when you get here."

"Great," I said sarcastically.

"What's that for?"

"Colin, the only time I meet you anywhere is to have drinks, dinner, or so you can show me a dead body."

"You're probably right, and just so you don't come under the wrong impression there's no dinner or drinks where I'm at."

Chapter 51

Nestled along the Cuyahoga River south of downtown, the Union Steel Yards were a long time past their glory days. Once filled with the activity of thousands of workers, the yards were now nothing more than barren land decorated with the rust of better times.

I followed Colin's directions down narrow roads and through gates left open by the hurried escape of the local economy. There was not a single sound and the desolation seemed to stretch beyond what I could have imagined. I was only five miles from the heart of Cleveland, but the only noise was the hum coming from my car's engine. There could have been no better place to find isolation in the metropolitan area.

It took me a couple of minutes to get my bearings and find Colin's car outside one of the remaining buildings. By the time I had a chance to park and unhook my seat belt he was already standing outside my door.

"Pretty quiet," I said getting out of the car and shutting the door behind me.

"Only ones here I would imagine."

"Where is the normal parade?" I had been picturing a scene like the one by the river with local cops, technicians, coroners, and people clamoring all over the place.

"The parade will come later. It's just you and me for right now." The obvious question must have been written on my face because Colin kept right on talking. "The call came on my personal cell phone."

"Did you get a chance to trace it?"

"No luck."

"I have to assume whoever it was that called you was the killer?"

Colin waved me on to walk with him and I followed him into the building. "He never admitted to the killing, but yeah I would assume it was him. The guy had a soft accent and it seemed to be East European, but there was a little something off with it."

"Off? You think we have a pretty good actor on our hands?"

"Could be."

"So why haven't you called in the local boys yet. It is their jurisdiction."

"Well that's the part that will keep you up at night," Colin said without one ounce of humor to his voice.

"Shit, what is it now?" As if I was sleeping much lately anyways.

"Well our mystery caller believes the C.P.D. will match the gun on the body to the one that shot Levi Zeitlin. He believes they'll run with it and close the file. Lack of resources... his words not mine."

"I could see that. Levi's murder needs to be solved, but the murder of his killer doesn't rate high on the priority list. Seems like good logic when you are dealing with the local police, but that still doesn't answer why you haven't called it in."

"Because the man on the phone insisted I bring you out here to have a look first."

"Me personally?"

"The one and only."

At that moment Colin stopped walking and I looked up to see a badly damage body hanging from the rafters of the building by his tied wrists. His feet had been severed and the wounds were being hungrily devoured by a swarm of flies. A few seagulls and crows were joining in on the rest of him. The stones and debris below the victim were covered in a large splatter pattern of blood. It looked like a Jackson Pollock. "Jimmy DeLuca," I asked Colin.

"Hard to tell, but that was my guess. My feeling is your girl Alex may want to watch herself."

Chapter 52

When the crime scene had been cleared and the story played out on the evening news, everything happened as expected. The headline story across all the local stations highlighted the murder of Levi Zeitlin, and each anchor seemed as pleased as the Cleveland Police that the killer had been found. Jimmy DeLuca's death was attributed to a drug deal gone wrong and the forensics team was waiting on a secondary ballistics test to confirm what everyone already seemed to know. The entire community seemed pleased with themselves having solved the murder of an important local socialite, and for getting a drug dealer off of the city's streets. Everyone but Daniel Shaw, who sat fuming in front of the television screens in his office.

He had been trying to call Kershaw to no avail and now Shaw sat staring blankly at the TVs. As Kershaw continued to ignore his phone calls, he became more certain it was intentional. The little shit was certainly hiding away somewhere trying to avoid Shaw's desire to strangle him.

Pacing across his office floor as he gazed at the view from his office window, Daniel Shaw began mumbling to himself trying to cover every angle and option to clean up the mess Kershaw had created. He began to wonder out loud how the killing of one little rich brat could have caused so much trouble for him. The entire blame had to be laid at the feet of Lee Kershaw. The man made one bad decision after another. The only reason he had been hired was so Shaw could keep his hands clean, but now as he looked down on them they appeared covered in shit.

The local police had predictably closed the case without snooping further into it. The Cleveland Police may have known better than to dig too deep into these matters, but Jack Francis and his FBI connections could care less whose feathers they ruffled. Damn old man Gilmore, Shaw should have had him shot for hiring Francis. At least someone had taken care of the greedy antique dealer. Charles Beard was a real moron for sticking his nose in matters he knew nothing about. So far the only good thing coming from all this was that a couple of true idiots were dead.

The phone on Shaw's desk began to ring so loud it appeared to want to leap onto the floor. The sound broke Shaw's thoughts sending him instantly into a more visible fit of rage.

"What?" The volume and ferociousness of Shaw's voice rattled through the phone.

The man at the other end spoke as he laughed. There was pure joy in his voice. "Rough night, Daniel? Personally I'm in quite a good mood. I found the evening news especially cheerful."

Shaw fell back into his chair, closed his eyes, and took a deep breath at the sound of the voice on the other end of the phone. "You," he said more calmly now. "You were behind all this."

The voice with the Midwestern accent chuckled. "Of course, did you really think your boy Kershaw was this incompetent?"

"How did you even know Kershaw and I were working with each other? Never mind, I don't really care at this point. Why don't you simply tell me what it's going to cost me to finish this mess and forget it ever existed?"

"You are not resigning that easy. Daniel you must know how you found yourself in this mess. I am very good at what I do, as I am sure you have already discovered, so when Lee Kershaw came to me to do your dirty work my greed took over smelling a golden goose to lay my golden egg."

"Your golden egg?"

"You are not that blind Daniel. You are my golden goose and my golden egg is going to be enough money to live off of for a very long time."

All of a sudden Shaw realized that the price for wanting Levi Zeitlin dead just got really expensive. "Why would I give you that kind of money when I don't even know who you are, other than being one hell of a son of a bitch?"

"Daniel, I have been so many people in so many places, that it really doesn't matter who I am today. All you simply must realize is what I am capable of, and today's news was only the beginning."

"I ought to kill your ass."

The man had a good laugh at Shaw's expense. "Now Daniel, that is no way to talk to your future business partner. Besides, who are you going to get to do it? I highly doubt Kershaw is capable, and you are not going to hire me to kill myself. Why that's simply ludicrous. Now Daniel let's be grownups. All you have to do is give me what I want and I will make all your dreams come true. It seems a simple and fair deal to me."

Daniel Shaw slumped deeper into the confines of his leather chair, beaten but still alive. "Fine I'll play along. What is it you want?"

"It is something very simple."

Chapter 53

I slathered a piece of rye bread with some soft butter as the sound of fish frying came from Colin's kitchen. With a beer in one hand and a pair of tongs in the other, Katya stood over a cast iron skillet as the oil bubbled and splattered onto the stove top. Not allowed anywhere near the cooking food, Colin and I sat at the table salivating at the aroma of the frying fish.

"Can't you wait until the food is ready?" Colin said to me as I shoved the bread into my mouth.

"Too hungry," I managed to mumble as I stuffed down the piece of rye. Colin shook his head and got up from the table grabbing a pair of cold beers from the fridge. Like a beer commercial, the sweat dripping off of the cold glass bottle was making my mouth water. "Have you thought anymore about what I should do next?" I asked having swallowed the last of the bread, and reached for a beer.

"I'm not on this case so figure it out for yourself."

"Thanks for the help," I went back to work on another piece of bread. "I was thinking my only hope may be to push Alex. The way I see it Jimmy's murder will have one of two effects on her." I took a bite of bread and swig of the cold beer, pausing for a moment to see if Colin would join the conversation. "The way I have it figured is it will either close her mouth tighter than it already is, and she'll go into hiding, or..."

"I'm going with that option," Colin interrupted.

"Or," I continued, "she's going to look at Jimmy's murder as a bounty on her head. Keeping her mouth shut now won't save her, especially if someone is cleaning house."

"So what's your plan then? Are you going to play the guardian angel and take her in under your protection, provide her with some comfort, and then hope she spills everything to you?"

"I doubt anyone can really protect Alex, but yeah that's my plan. Last time I checked, you hadn't brought anything better to the table."

"He never does," Katya said setting a plate of fish down in front of us and a bowl of homemade tartar sauce. "Let's eat."

There was silence at the table for a few minutes as everyone began to devour the food. Colin wiped some bread from around his mouth and finally spoke. "You sure that bringing Alex closer to you is the best plan you've got?" Katya and I looked up from over our plates. "Alex knows who hired Kershaw and so did Jimmy DeLuca. I'm also pretty sure that's why the young man is dead and missing his feet."

"Hey, I'm eating here," Katya yelled.

"Sorry," Colin continued. "If you can get her to tell you who is behind the killings then we may be able to find a motive. A motive would help put a quick end to the whole mess. Hell, maybe we can get lucky and Alex can give us the motive too."

"I'm sure Alex knows something, but that's hoping for a lot." I was having trouble figuring out how serious Colin was taking our conversation.

"Well she'll at least point the figure at Kershaw, and I bet Kershaw hired Jimmy to kill Levi Zeitlin."

"Are you really trying to help or just amuse yourself?"

"What?" Colin asked innocently.

"Of course Alex will point us towards Kershaw, but we already know about Kershaw's involvement. What we don't know is how he is involved. I need to know who hired him."

"I'm simply saying that if Alex wants to point the finger at Kershaw, we can bring him in with her as a witness. Once we've brought him in maybe he'll talk."

"Colin you've been with the Feds way too long. There is no way Alex is going to play the witness, and there is no way Kershaw is going to be a rat."

"Oh, I think Kershaw would play the rat, but you are probably right about Alex. She won't even talk to you." Colin cleaned his plate and stood up from the table.

"You know there is one thing we are forgetting."

"What's that?" he asked putting his plate in the dishwasher.

"The other player."

"The other player?" Katya asked finishing up her dinner as well.

I didn't need to answer her, Colin beat me to it.

"The other player. The person who put the body in Chelsea's trunk, and the person who killed Jimmy DeLuca. The man with the funny accent who called my cell phone to tell me all about it."

Chapter 54

Fearing for her life, Alex had already begun to keep a low profile. Now she sat on my couch in a state of pure fear and was a nervous wreck. The strong confident woman who once could frighten me was now a mere shell of her former self. I had somehow gotten lucky and had the unfortunate task of telling her about Jimmy. She had somehow missed all the attention from the news on the murder, which was a surprise to me since the whole town was talking about it. Now the woman who was always cool and calm was downing her bourbon faster than a college kid on game day. I gave her a few minutes to collect herself as I refilled both of our whiskey glasses before asking her any questions. By the time I came back with new drinks she was taking deep breaths and gathering her thoughts.

"What is your next move?" I asked.

She took a moment to answer trying to regain some strength in her voice. "I don't know maybe I should just run."

"Can you afford to?"

"For a little while, might be long enough for everything to blow over."

"Do you really believe whoever killed Jimmy will simply forget about you?" She might have a slim shot if she ran, but I needed her to believe that it was an option better left untaken.

"Probably not," Alex answered disappointedly. "What should I do Jack?" She almost broke down again. Seeing her like this reminded me of an animal backed into a corner. Right now she was on the defensive, but if you kept pushing her back eventually she was going to attack.

"Tell me everything Alex, and I mean every little detail this time. Let Colin and I hunt these people down so you can go back to living your life. It's really your only option. Do you want to spend the rest of your life running from shadows?" There it was, out there, and now it was all up to Alex.

"Keeping my mouth shut was supposed to keep me safe, but now with Jimmy dead I have to believe those days are over." Alex's voice was getting stronger and I could sense a little fire returning to her now that she was feeling a little less helpless. "A lot of things are starting to make sense to me now," she continued. "I had lunch with Kershaw the other day and he was acting a little peculiar."

"How's that?"

"He had a loose tongue, which is quite unusual for him. He also seemed a little on edge, but that could have been because he was dressed like a moron in the summer heat. Either way he was acting very uncharacteristic of himself."

"You said he had a loose tongue. What was it he was telling you?"

"Nothing I hadn't already figured out for myself."

"Come on Alex, quit beating around the bush. I'm trying to help you remember."

"Alright, but the role of the rat doesn't fit me very well."

"Will a pine box fit you better, because it's looking more and more like your only other option." I needed to be tough on her. She was playing on a side she had never expected to be on and it made her feel uncomfortable.

"Take it easy on me Jack. I'm going to tell you everything I know, but first I need to know that you'll protect me."

"I promise."

"Good now come here." Alex stood up and grabbed my hand pulling me from where I sat. The woman I knew as Alex had apparently fully returned.

"What are you doing," I asked, but from the look on her face I already knew the answer.

"I am afraid for my life Jack, so what do you think I'm doing? I'm making sure I get to have sex one last time." We got to my bedroom and she pushed me down on the bed before slowly climbing on top of me. "Better be at the top of your game, remember this might be my last time."

Chapter 55

With everything happening so quickly since the murder of Jimmy DeLuca I had become distracted. I was also getting worn down and it was obviously causing me to lose my edge, after all, I had completely forgotten about the Gilmores for the past couple of days.

When your phone rings at two in the morning it is never going to be a good call. My mother always said nothing good ever happens after midnight, and as I got older I had realized she was right. Alex was in bed next to me when my phone vibrated on the dresser. She had no response to the noise, having fallen into a deep sleep from the combination of fear, bourbon, and some of the best sex I was capable of. I got up to grab my cell and found a text message waiting for me. It was simple, demanding, and to the point. *Need to talk now* was all it read. Everything in my gut told me to ignore it and I should have.

Before the clock struck three I was dressed and made it down to the casino without ever waking Alex. I now stood by the main entrance of the brightly lit building waiting for Madeline to show up. The woman was intriguing, frightening, and an incredible turn-on when she wanted to be. The last one was probably the reason I was willing to wait in the middle of the night on a street corner for her. The fact that Madeline had chosen Daniel Shaw's casino as the meeting place was more than a little interesting after finally having my conversation with Alex.

The valet pulled up in front driving a familiar silver Mercedes as Madeline came walking out the front door of the casino. "Get in" was all I got from her as she walked around to the driver's side door. I followed obediently and she speed off with her recognizable squeal of the tires. I was beginning to believe it was the only way she knew how to drive. Within seconds we were speeding down Ontario and heading towards the I-90 ramp.

"Where are we going?" I asked. She looked at me and then turned on the radio as a sign she was in no mood to talk to me. On her terms as always, I should have been prepared for that. We finally pulled off of the highway a little after four in the morning near the small lake town of Huron. Madeline quickly pulled into a gas station right off the highway before she finally spoke to me.

"Fill it up for me will you?" handing me her card, "and grab some beer from inside."

"Please." I said, a little annoyed with the woman and feeling like I had been kidnapped by her.

"Please," she responded with a small seductive smile.

I did everything I was told and got back into the car without another word from Madeline. Within minutes of our stop, we were speeding back down the highway heading west.

"Madeline, I'm beginning to feel like I've been kidnapped. Can you at least talk to me or tell me where we are going?"

"I'm taking you someplace where the two of us can be alone and talk. Until then, I would prefer the silence."

"Where are we going?" I asked a little more sternly hoping my annoyance with the situation would persuade her to talk.

"When's the last time you've been to South Bass Island?"

"I went to Put-in-Bay for the Fourth of July and the island was packed with crazy college kids."

"Well have no worries there won't be crazy college kids where we're heading. My father has an old house on the east point of the island. It is quiet, but close enough to the town if we want to get a little crazy."

"Why bring me all the way out here simply to talk?"

"Jack we never get to talk in private, and back in the city there are too many distractions. If you ever want to get this whole mess behind you, we'll need some time alone. A little time on the island with me will be a great distraction from your case." Madeline gave me her best smile, and suddenly I was feeling a little guilty for leaving Alex in the middle of the night. Part of me was also excited about my prospects.

Chapter 56

The man knew his work on Jimmy DeLuca was brilliant. He smiled at the lasting image it must have left on Jack Francis as he looked at the bound wrists and spattering blood all across God's precious earth. He also felt good knowing he had played Daniel Shaw to perfection. Half of his promised money was already deposited into his account and transferred across a multitude of banks in the Caribbean. The other half would come as soon as he kept his part of the bargain. It was time to go back to work.

Outside of Jack Francis' condo building the man sat sipping a slightly chilled burgundy at a wine bar. He knew Alex was inside too afraid to come out of hiding. He had more than enough skill to slip into the place unnoticed and do the job, but where was the beauty in that. His battle wouldn't end with the simple killing of Alex, no he was preparing for the grand finale. It wasn't in this woman's nature to be caged and he knew with the right motivation she would come out on her own.

He paid for his wine in cash and moved towards the front door of the condo building. Before he got to the front entrance he was greeted by a pimple-faced doorman, who swung the door open wide giving him ample room to proceed if he had wanted to.

"Thanks, but I'm not going in," he said with his Midwestern accent, "but you can still help me with something."

"Sure, what is it?" the kid asked enthusiastically.

The man took a note out from the inner pocket of his jacket and handed it to the doorman along with a twenty. "It is very important Jack Francis receives this. He's out of town at the moment, but he has a young woman who is staying with him. Take it up to her and stress the importance of Jack receiving it the moment he returns. Can you manage that for me?"

The young doorman looked at the note and then at the twenty in his hands. "Sure thing, I'll do it right away sir. Did you want me to leave your name with the young lady?"

"No its OK, Jack will know who it's from when he gets it." The man smiled as he walked back down the street. A small skip developed in his step. A few more days and he could leave Cleveland with all the money he had ever needed.

Chapter 57

Standing with her back to the closed door of the condo, Alex stared down at the note in her hands. It could be nothing she thought, but Jack disappearing in the middle of the night already had her flustered. With everything around her seemingly tumbling into an open grave, she was concerned for her safety more than ever before, and in the business she was in, there were plenty of reasons to worry. "Probably just a note from another resident of the building," she said out loud to herself in a reassuring voice. Alex tossed the note onto the counter and went for the phone in Jack's living room. She scrolled through the caller ID until the number she was looking for came up. Calling Agent Colin Sommers was really not something she wanted to do, but if anyone knew where Jack was he would.

The phone rang three times before Colin answered. "What is it Jack?"

"It's not Jack," Alex said sheepishly.

"Who is this," Colin began with annoyance before realizing. "Oh, it must be the lovely Alex I've heard so much about."

"Yeah, sorry to bother you but I thought you might be able to help me."

"No problem."

"I was wondering if you've heard from Jack at all today?"

"Can't say that I have. Why, did he not come home last night?" There was a little bit of sarcasm to the agent's voice.

"He was here, but he left sometime in the middle of the night. I'm not sure when."

"Jack has been known to leave a woman in the middle of the night before, but never at his own house," Colin joked but Alex seemed to be oblivious. "Alex, are you alright?"

"I'm not the type a girl who usually worries. Usually, I'm the one sneaking out in the middle of the night, but with Jimmy's murder I'm a little on edge."

"I'm sorry, I'll try to keep my jokes to myself then. Getting back to Jack, I haven't heard from him and I don't really have any idea where he might have gone. Did you try his cell?"

"I never thought to try his cell first. Sorry, I'm not thinking straight. I'm probably not using my head at all."

"It's OK Alex. Relax a bit and calm your nerves. I'm sure you'll be able to reach him on his cell."

"You're probably right," Alex said calmly and feeling a bit ridiculous.

"Alex."

"Yeah?"

"Can you do me a favor?" Colin asked.

"Sure, what is it?"

"When you get a hold of Jack, and find out where he ran off to, have him call me will you?"

"Anything important you want me to tell him?"

"No, but let him know that it's important that he calls me."

"Anything else?" Alex asked.

"Nope that should do it. Alex do yourself a favor, and get your nerves together. From what Jack said you're a smart cookie when you have your wits about you. Also, if you want my advice, I would keep a low profile. It would probably be best if you didn't leave Jack's place for a while."

"Thanks for telling me I need to calm down and then reminding me that my life may be in danger."

"Sorry, I didn't mean to scare you, just to keep you safe."

"I know Colin."

"Take care Alex," and he hung up the phone.

Alex set the phone down and gazed out the window into the city for a few minutes. She began to wonder who Daniel Shaw would send to kill her. Somewhere out there somebody was waiting for her to make a mistake. The fear she was feeling for the first time in her life was hampering her and causing her judgment to falter. She knew if she didn't find a way to manage her emotions, sooner or later, she would make a deadly mistake, and most of all, she needed to figure out how to get control of her life back.

Seeing the note on the counter, Alex walked over and grabbed it and headed back to Jack's bedroom. "That son of a bitch better answer," she said grabbing her cell phone on the table next to the bed. Alex dialed Jack's number in a fury and waited for an answer.

Chapter 58

The porch overlooked a small stretch of pristine water, where sailboats raced in the morning sun, stretching out over neighboring Kelleys Island. My pot of coffee was down to the murky, cold, bottom residue and there was still no stirring from Madeline's room. We arrived at the ferry dock an hour early for the first crossing, and spent our time waiting at a small diner with a parade of fisherman moving in and out in search of their morning coffee. By the time we finally made it to the Gilmore's island home, the two of us parted ways in search of some much needed rest. Sleep had come over me almost instantly when I laid my head down in one of the guestrooms, but it didn't have the courtesy to stick around long. In another room of the house Madeline appeared to be having no trouble avoiding the morning, and it would seem she planned on spending a good part of the afternoon in bed. She seemed to love keeping me waiting even though she was the one who wanted to talk. She was either wasting my time, or her news was so bad, she was trying to work herself up to tell me.

My patience waiting for Madeline had finally expired, and I tossed the cold sludge at the bottom of my mug over the porch. I found my way back into the room I had slept in and did my best to freshen up with a cold shower and one of the guest toothbrushes from the medicine cabinet. My only choice in clothes were the ones I had been wearing the night before, so I threw them on grudgingly and made my way back downstairs. I felt the need to get out of the house and explore the island in search of food and more suitable attire. I decided not to wake Madeline to go with me, and I made my way to the old horse barn that was now used as the property's garage.

Inside, a golf cart was parked next to Madeline's Mercedes, and the keys were hanging from the wall next to the door. Golf carts were better suited for the island lifestyle and the steady cruising speed was a perfect way to catch the sites. On the way into town, I was kept cool by the breeze off of Lake Erie as I passed groups of tourists traveling on bikes. The small town of Put-in-Bay was situated around a large park, which overlooked a bay full of boats. The three main roads surrounding the park housed a variety of tourist traps, restaurants, and enough bars to rival Key West. I found a spot to park the golf cart and headed into one of the shops to add some clothes to my small wardrobe. To me standard island attire consists of a pair of swim trunks, a t-shirt, and sandals.

I was feeling pretty good with my new clothes and was checking out of the store when Madeline finally called me. The phone in my pocket vibrated and vibrated and I simply ignored it. Instead, I sauntered down to the waterfront and out to a pier stretching into the bay. On the pier was assortment of food stands and I was sure there would be something suitable for my lunch. Within minutes I had found myself a perch sandwich, a cold beer, and a seat where I could watch the sailboats bob up and down on their moorings. For the first time since Madeline kidnapped me I was starting to think getting out of the city was a good idea.

Chapter 59

Walking beneath the shaded trees of the park I took my time enjoying the sweetness of summer on the island. My love affair with life was cut short with the vibrating cell phone in my pocket. I could only assume it was Madeline calling again, and I had a strong urge to ignore the call one more time, but instead my curiosity won out. I pulled the phone from my pocket and took a seat on the edge of a fountain before I decided to answer.

"Hello."

"Jack, where are you?"

Shit, it was Alex. I had nearly forgotten about having left her in the middle of the night. "Alex, sorry I had to take off like that in the middle of the night, but something came up. Are you alright?"

"I'm fine, doing better than I was last night anyways. Waking up to find you missing this morning didn't help though."

I was beginning to wonder if I had found myself suddenly in a serious relationship with this woman. The thought was frightening and a little intriguing. "I'm really sorry about that. I got a message in the middle of the night and it was a lead I needed to look into. I would have woken you up, but you were out cold and after the night you had, I figured sleep was the best option." It was almost the truth. "I had to leave town for a day, two at the most, but I'll be back as soon as I can."

"Anything good?" she asked.

"I'm not sure yet, but it's something I need to look into further."

"Mind telling me a little bit more? Maybe I can help connect some dots for you."

Suddenly Alex opens up to me and now all she wants to do is help. It might have been better before. "It's nothing we need to be discussing over the phone." I had to keep the call as vague as possible because even though I hadn't done anything wrong, there was no reason to provoke a woman already on the edge. "We'll go over everything when I get back."

"I guess that makes sense. By the way, the doorman brought a note by for you. Oh, and before I forget, you need to get in touch with Colin. It sounded like it was important. Wow, I'm beginning to sound like your secretary. I think we need to get me out of your condo soon. I do not play the secretary role very well."

"Seems like you have it down to me."

"Shut up."

"I'm kidding. Did Colin mention anything about what he wanted?"

"Not a word. The man's all hush hush just like you."

"Guess I'll have to call him." With Colin it could be anything. I was hoping it had to do with the case, but with him it could just as easily be an invite to happy hour. "What did the note say?"

"I have no idea. It seemed a little inappropriate for me to read it."

"Well that was polite of you," I said, "but if you're going to make it as my secretary you need to be a little nosier. The good ones always are."

"I am no one's secretary, Jack Francis. Now do you want me to read it to you or are you going to keep on making jokes?" Alex asked in the tone of a scolding school teacher.

"Go ahead and read it to me." I had no idea what it could possibly be about, but I had to assume there was nothing in it that would get me in trouble with Alex. With Madeline here on the island the main trouble maker was out of play. Also, with Alex having been so open to me lately I had to show a little trust in her as well.

"Alright, give me a second." I could hear her rummaging around with the phone. "Got it, are you ready?"

"Go ahead."

"Files on a computer stay on a computer, even after you delete them. To find them, all you need is the proper tools."

"Is that all?" I asked.

"No it's signed...sort of."

"Well, are you going to tell me?"

"Just trying to help."

"I know you are, but can you read me the rest?" I said, sounding a little too bossy.

"You're an idiot Jack. I did read it to you. It is signed 'just trying to help'."

"Oh," I said feeling a little bad for being short with her. I thought for a few minutes leaving silence over the phone.

"Any ideas?" Alex asked hopefully.

"Actually I do have one. I really don't like the idea of a mysterious note coming to my front door, but it does make a really good point."

"Why not try and fill me in, because I'm lost."

I was pretty sure I had the note's meaning right on. It was apparently simple, too simple. "There are programs out there that can retrieve deleted files from a computer's memory. Items deleted are actually not removed from the computer, but instead they become inaccessible to the users of the computer. I'm sure the point the note is trying to make, is the photos Charles Beard had of Chelsea are probably still on his computer. That's if he ever put them on there in the first place."

"Didn't you check his computer before?"

"Not really."

"Is the retrieval program something you need to get from your FBI buddies?" Alex was intrigued.

"No, they are pretty common and easy to download right off of the internet."

"Jack."

"What is it?"

"You need to come home soon," Alex's voice did nothing to hide that she was excited about the breakthrough. "I'm feeling like a caged bird and this could be our opportunity to finally bring everything to an end. We need to get a look at Beard's computer."

"I'll be back as soon as I can, but first I need to call Colin back."

Chapter 60

"I need to get off the island," I told Madeline the moment I got back to the house. My phone call with Colin only furthered my need to get back to the city, as if Alex's call had already not been enough. Colin's search for Levi Zeitlin's phone records had gathered some interesting information, which pointed directly at Daniel Shaw, just as Alex had indicated. Colin felt there was a lot more to my case and it appeared to be quickly heating up. There wasn't much more Madeline could add and I was wasting my time sitting on the island with her.

"Relax a little Jack," Madeline said getting up from the spot on the back deck where she had been sunning herself. Her long, tanned legs only looked longer and more seductive by the skimpy two piece she had on. "We haven't had a chance to talk or a moment of each other's company."

"Normally, I would be completely willing to spend a few days on the island."

"With me?"

I looked at the beautiful woman who stood before me and the look in her eyes told me we both knew the answer. "Madeline, I really need to get back to the city. There have been some new developments and I need to pursue them immediately." I had no desire to break the news about Chelsea's photos being retrieved off of Beard's computer, but if I had to play that card I would.

"Why don't you tell me about them, and I'll decide how important they are."

"Madeline I have no time for your childish games. You brought me here to talk so why don't you start talking before I decide to swim home." My patience had run out and my voice resonated with approaching anger.

"Come on, I'm hungry." Madeline walked right past me and into the house. She pulled a bottle of chilled chardonnay from the wine cooler and then a plate of charcuterie from the fridge. Wrapping a towel around her bottom half, she took the wine and food out onto the front porch overlooking the lake. "Jack I forgot the wine glasses. Be a dear will you?"

I searched the kitchen for the glasses and came back out onto the porch to find Madeline sitting in an Adirondack, snacking on some Serrano ham. I poured some wine for the both of us and sat down next to her. "Can we talk now?"

"Most men who are alone with a half-naked woman would want to do a lot of things, but I doubt talking would be on that list."

"Normally, I would be most men. Normally, we would take the wine to the bedroom and only come out for more, but not today. There is nothing normal about this whole mess, from your sister to the murders. Now please, what is it you want to talk about?

"If you insist, but I liked your bedroom idea better."

"Maybe next time," I said, not amused.

"Jack, I brought you out here because Chelsea killed Charles Beard and my father had it cleaned up."

Chapter 61

After hanging up with Jack, Alex discovered she was brimming with a renewed sense of confidence and hope. There was a sudden eagerness to be proactive with her situation and she had no intention of being helpless any longer.

In a room down the hall from Jack's bedroom, Alex found a small, crowded office. Inside was a disorganized desk and a dusty computer. An array of file boxes littered the floor with good intentions of updating them to the digital age. Alex made her way through the mess and sat down at the desk as she powered up the computer. She had to hope Jack at least had an internet connection even though the desktop appeared to be rarely used. When the computer finally booted up, she saw there was a network connection, and it was only a matter of minutes before she a found a multitude of links to the software she was looking for. For a man who barely used his office, he certainly had a grasp on technology, Alex thought.

A majority of the file retrieval programs appeared to be pretty straight forward and designed for the average home user. Alex took a little time to read a few reviews before selecting a program to download. She needed to be able to download the program and work through it with some ease, if she was going to be able to go through Charles Beard's computer quickly. To satisfy her curiosity, she went through a few of Jack's files in search of an item to delete and retrieve. Knowing the files on Beard's computer were probably picture files, Alex chose a nice picture of Jack fishing to use as practice. After finishing the installation process for the retrieval software, she deleted the photo of Jack and put the program to work. Alex was amazed at how many files came back when the program finished its search. There was no doubt that delete really did not mean delete, something she would have to remember in the future.

The amount of returned queries was too enormous for her to sift through, so she narrowed the search with the self-explained advanced search tool. When the requested files returned to the screen, the jpeg of Jack fishing was at the top of the list. Alex could only hope the photos of Levi Zeitlin's murder would be as easy to find on Beard's computer. It made sense assuming the computer had not been used since the antique dealer's death.

The rush of excitement stemming from the simplicity of the retrieval process almost concealed the fear she had over the note Jack had received. If the note was a trap, it was a trap meant for Jack, Alex concluded. Whoever sent it had their own motivations and reasons to bait Jack into going to Beard's house in search of the files, but Alex felt some of the risk could be avoided if she went instead of Jack. There was no doubt in her mind it was dangerous for her to leave the condo after Jimmy's murder, but the risk was worth the reward. Alex's mind was already processing the angles she could play with those photos in her possession and they all told her to go after Beard's computer as soon as possible. Even with the strong possibility of a trap waiting to spring at Beard's home, she had to assume it was there waiting for Jack and not her. He was the obvious target, and besides, no one knew where she was and if they did, then she would already be dead.

With all the will Alex could muster after the past couple of days, she knew it was time to do something on her own, time for her to remove her name from the hit list, and take back control of her life. Alex had enough of being afraid and was tired of the threat of Daniel Shaw's retribution.

Chapter 62

When the initial request for the Levi Zeitlin's phone records came back the only information Colin received was for the Bratenahl home. It was an obvious mistake and irritated him for the sheer simplicity of it. Everything at the Zeitlin home was still registered in Levi's father's name so there was no reason for the mix up. Colin resent the request specifically detailing that he wanted Levi Zeitlin's cell phone records, spelling it out to his subordinates as well as he possibly could. When the second request came back it returned two different numbers for the young man and instantly Colin was intrigued.

The first cell phone number, which Colin had to assume was Levi's main source of communication, came back with a long and tedious list of numbers. Most of the calls could be traced to kids his own age and social group. There were a few numbers traced back to a more sinister lot, but Colin knew the connection was the high-end drug world. There was seldom a group of wealthy kids with a large amount of money and time on their hands, who didn't end up with some kind of drug habit. The final group of numbers Colin picked out could be associated directly to Jack's case, all of them belonging to the Gilmores. Colin was surprised by the amount of calls between Levi and Madeline though, thinking Chelsea's number would have appeared more often.

While the first cell phone was a little curious, the second one was a gold mine. Most of the time when a person has a second phone it was either supplied by their work or used for unpublicized habits, like an affair. The most prominent number on the call list was to a cell phone traced out to Rocky River and belonged to Willow Shaw. Colin checked a little further into the background of the Shaws and found out that everything Mrs. Shaw owned from her BMW to her credit cards, were all under the name of her husband, Daniel Shaw. The man had complete control over his wife, except for one little cell phone in her name. The last call between Levi and Willow Shaw came on the night of Levi's murder. The curious thing was the phone had been used after that.

Impressively enough on the night Levi was being pulled from the Cuyahoga River, he managed to reach out and call someone. Colin had a complete understanding of what it meant. It meant whoever put Levi in Chelsea's trunk managed to grab the kid's most precious cell phone as well. All the blame may have been laid on Jimmy DeLuca, but Colin knew better after having visited Jimmy in the steelyard. The last number dialed out by Levi's phone gave Colin even more cause to believe someone was playing games. The call had been made to Daniel Shaw. There was a small chance Jimmy DeLuca had made the call to inform Shaw that Levi's body had been found, but Colin felt if Jimmy had possession of Levi's phone, it would have been destroyed before his body came out of the river. Plus, DeLuca would have called Kershaw instead of Daniel Shaw directly. There was someone else at work here, someone with a little more bravado than Jimmy DeLuca. Colin had to believe the phone call had not been pleasant for Shaw, and wondered if maybe blackmail was on the menu once again.

Chapter 63

"Hold on a second, Madeline." I had thought the case had run out of surprises, but to think little Chelsea Gilmore had pulled the trigger on Charles Beard was really something. "Why don't you back up a little bit and tell me everything." Another normally tight lipped woman was suddenly about to spill her guts to me and it was a little hard to believe my luck. Maybe my stars were finally in line.

"I had no idea Chelsea had it in her," Madeline began calmly. "She has always been a little unstable though."

"Your father mentioned that."

"Maybe it was because Mother died giving birth to her, but I don't really know. Anyways Father must have realized how unstable she had become because he was having her followed all the time."

"Who was it?"

"Probably one of his hired thugs, but I'm not sure who. The only reason I found out about it was because I overheard him and Douglas discussing it. It really is amazing how much I have learned from my bedroom porch."

"Tell me about it. I seem to remember you using the same technique on me," I said thinking about my first meeting with Captain Gilmore.

"What can I say? Old habits die hard. Still, I had no idea Father was worried about Chelsea killing someone. I assumed he simply wanted her watched."

"You were with me in the car the night Beard was shot, so how did you find out Chelsea had pulled the trigger?"

"When I got home that night I poked my head into Chelsea's room to check on her, since she had been so upset over the blackmail. When I looked in she was asleep and seemed fine. There was only one thing that worried me, a bottle of sleeping pills next to her bed. Normally, I would not have thought too much about it but my sister's stress levels were at an all-time high and I was afraid she might take too many."

"Hold on, you're telling me you believed Chelsea was unstable enough to overdose on sleeping pills, but not to shoot someone?"

"Pills were more Chelsea's style," Madeline said. "The next day my sister spent the afternoon in her room crying, talking to herself, and pacing the floor. Not an uncommon habit of late. Finally I had enough and went to try to calm her down, but her room suddenly became quiet as I approached her door. I turned back towards my room assuming she had cried herself to sleep like a small child, but I was wrong. A few minutes later I found her on my bed waiting for me as I came out of the shower."

"And that's when she told you," I asked wanting to keep the story moving.

"Yes. The poor thing was a wreck. Either father noticed Chelsea's condition or his man filled him in on everything, because the next day he shipped her off to a clinic in New York."

"So that's why you said Chelsea had said everything she was going to, because your father sent her off to a psych ward."

Madeline gave her head a little shake. "I'm not sure what the place is. Maybe it's a psych ward but probably some type of rehab clinic if I know father."

"What I can't seem to figure out is why you are so willing to tell me all of this now. Beard's body is still missing and your father has the blackmail pictures of Chelsea, so why would you tell anyone at all?"

"Jack, I told you from the very beginning that I would do anything to protect my sister."

"I'm still not following."

"The man hired to follow Chelsea bothers me. He is a loose end."

"Why does everyone need to tie up loose ends? I'm pretty sure that is how this whole mess started."

"Appearances are everything in my world Jack. It's important that the Gilmore family appears perfect even though we are far from it. Besides, there's more if you are willing to listen."

I sure did, because a week ago nobody was talking to me, and now Madeline was setting up her sister for murder.

Chapter 64

When Madeline began again she started to think outside of the box and into a realm I should have been exploring. She was certainly focused on protecting her sister, but she was seeing the bigger picture.

"I began to think back and retrace events," Madeline said. "Chelsea's confession should have screwed me all up, but instead it made me more determined to protect her. I had no choice but to try to keep my head clear."

I sat there silent for a moment not wanting to interrupt her, but she got lost in her own thoughts. "Explain it to me."

"Here is the thing, the night we had dinner at the club I was approached in my car by a man."

"Do you know who it was?"

"Not really. He was in my backseat, and it was dark, so I couldn't get a good look at him from my mirror. On the other hand, he did have the blackmailer's photos of Chelsea and gave them to me willingly, before disappearing back into the night. It finally dawned on me that the man in my backseat had to have been the one father hired to follow Chelsea."

"Why do you think that?" I asked, coming to the same conclusion.

"Why else would he have the photos and give them up so easily?"

"It makes sense, except I ran into the house only a moment after we heard the shots. How did he get a hold of the evidence when it was missing before I got there?"

Madeline smiled, "The evidence left the house mere seconds before you arrived."

"Chelsea," I said a little confused.

"Yep, even in her frantic state she was able to still find what she had been after."

"But then how did this other guy happen to get them?"

"I'm still working on that part," Madeline said.

I wasn't because I already had figured that part out. "How do you know Chelsea got what she wanted from Beard?"

"After father sent her away I did what any good sister would do and I went through her stuff."

"Why?"

"I was looking for the gun. It was the only thing connecting her with Beard's death if he ever turns up."

"So did you find it?"

"No," Madeline said frustrated, "but I did come across a memory card."

"Alright some of this is coming together and parts are still a little confusing, but this is what I know. Today I received a note at my condo. I'm now going to bet the house that whoever sent me that note was also the same person in the backseat of your car." Even though Alex said no name was on the note I had a hunch it was Colin's buddy who called in the DeLuca murder. "The note told me how to get my hands on copies of Chelsea's photos. I will almost guarantee it is how your guy ended up with them that night after you left the club."

"How?" Madeline asked curiously.

"Beard's computer, but it's hard to explain how." It would have been easier to tell her but the last thing I needed was Madeline heading over to Beard's home. "I have one more question for you."

"Go on."

"You said your father cleaned up Beard's death, how?"

"I'm sorry, but it was nothing more than an assumption, but I have to assume father's hired help watched the house until you left and then came in and cleaned up. It's the only reasonable answer since he was hired to look after Chelsea."

"It was a pretty impressive clean up in such a short period of time. I think your father's hired help is a little too skilled for someone hired to simply watch over your sister."

Chapter 65

What little patience Alex had was quickly disappearing, between Jack's middle of the night escapades, and her feeling like a caged bird inside his condo. There was only so much she could take before something would have to be done about her present situation. Even the threat on her life wasn't enough for her to ignore the potential opportunity in finding those files on Beard's computer, and having a little leverage with Daniel Shaw. They could even be used to play Captain Gilmore if she wanted. Two of the city's most powerful men connected by a simple photograph brought with it a lot of possibilities to whoever was willing to take a little risk. With Alex's life already on the line it took most of the risk out of the equation.

While she was lying on the couch in one of Jack's dress shirts, she realized it was time for her to do something. Sitting around and waiting on the help of other people was simply not her style. Moving quickly she went to the bedroom, pulled off Jack's shirt and tossed it on the bed. The shower was cold and revitalized her body from the lethargic day of doing nothing. Once she was ready, she called a cab and headed down to the street, a woman on a mission.

A debate had been raging through her mind when she showered. Part of her knew that going straight to Charles Beard's house to retrieve the files from his computer might be the safest bet, but if someone was there waiting, for Jack or whoever else might show up, then Alex would be going in blind and unarmed. She already felt helpless enough over the past few days, so she directed the cabby to head towards her apartment. It was a risk but she needed some protection, and until Jack returned, all she had was her gun.

Grabbing the Bersa Thunder from her closet lock box, Alex realized that she had forgotten a way to save the files found on Beard's computer. Stowing the pistol, she made her way back down to the street, and walked a few blocks to a small electronics store where she bought a small flash drive for her key chain, and a second one to hide as a backup. Paying the man behind the counter in cash, Alex was finally ready to make her way across town to the antique dealer's house.

The streets seemed suddenly deserted, and she had to go a couple blocks before she was able to hail a cab. The drive across the bridge spanning the crooked waters of the Cuyahoga was painless and congestion free. Alex had the cab driver drop her off in the market district of Ohio City, not wanting anyone to know where she was going. It might have been a little walk to Beard's home, but it was certainly better than a nosy cab driver.

Leaving the driver a healthy tip, Alex pretended to window shop as she watched him drive off. The moment the cab was out of view, she began her walk into the Ohio City neighborhood unaware of a new cab pulling onto the street behind her.

Chapter 66

"I can't believe that little spoiled brat had it in her," Colin said from the bar at the Greenhouse Tavern. Madeline and I had raced back to Cleveland almost immediately after our conversation. "Do you believe her?" he asked me.

"There is no reason not to. Madeline has been hard to pin down in the past, but I doubt she would call her sister a killer if it wasn't true."

"The rich play different games than we do. What did you think about those phone records?" Colin asked knowing full well our conclusions would be the same.

We had gone over them the moment I got to the bar and I continued to pour over each page as we talked. "I'm pretty sure Levi's cell phones are telling us a good story here, and probably offering us a motive if my assumptions are right."

"So what are you planning on doing with the information?" He asked as he shoveled a fork full of gravy covered fries into his mouth.

"Nothing. The phone records prove to me that Alex was correct about Daniel Shaw being behind the shooting, but it is not enough to hold up legally, especially when we got a hold of them illegally."

"Maybe you should talk to Willow Shaw. I'm sure she is overcome with emotion by the loss of her young lover."

"And probably scared to death she'll be next. I'll talk to her in the morning. What I need to do is get Lee Kershaw to talk. He took the orders from Shaw and passed them on for execution. Kershaw would also know who was sent to kill Jimmy, which I assume is your caller and the author of my recent note."

Colin smiled at me with a look that said *good luck buddy*.

"Kershaw has no reason to talk to you."

"No, but I think he'll start to open up if he thinks his life is in jeopardy. It worked with Alex didn't it?"

"Sure, get the man to see his maker in the near future and we will have this thing all wrapped up."

"I think we can keep the maker out of it. We do want him alive to testify someday." I reached over and stole one of Colin's fries.

"What's your plan then?" he asked with a look that told me I would lose my hand if I attempted a stunt like that again.

"I'm working on it. There has been a lot to process in the past twenty-four hours."

"You've still got your little note to deal with too."

"Thanks for the reminder Colin. You know you can be so helpful on occasion."

"I'm here for you buddy."

I was tired from the past day's excursion and needed to check on Alex. I had been sitting at the bar with Colin for a couple of hours now and my ass was numb from the stool. "I need to get home, it has been a sleepless couple of days."

"By all means don't let me keep you." Colin gestured towards the door sarcastically. "Go check in with the missus and tell her I said hi."

"You are real cute, you know that."

"Sure do. One more thing before you go, Jack."

"Make it quick, I'm tired."

"If Kershaw is the lynchpin to any case against Daniel Shaw then he is being watched closely, so you better be careful when you make your move on him."

"Now Colin, for once that is some good advice."

Chapter 67

All I wanted was a good night's sleep. If I could somehow get one restful night, I would be re-energized to deal with everything tomorrow and have a clear head to do it. On my walk home from my meeting with Colin I decided my long day entitled me to a small snack before bed. I had two choices according to my stomach and I was having trouble choosing between sushi and a sandwich. With Alex at the condo I figured the appropriate thing to do was to see if she was hungry as well. My home phone rang and rang until the sound of my own voice answered on the voicemail. I was not surprised Alex didn't pick up the phone. It was getting late and she had probably already retreated to the bedroom. My first instinct was to leave her alone if she had already gone to bed, but I had yet to call her since returning to town, and figured it was probably a good time to start apologizing for the night before. She had become accustomed to leaving her cell phone on a charger next to my bed, so I knew there was a good chance she would answer it.

It rang for a little longer than I would have liked before she answered with a whispered, "Hello?"

"Were you asleep?"

"No."

"I'm on my way home. I was thinking about picking up some food, are you hungry?"

"Jack, I'm not at your place at the moment." There was hesitation in her voice. "I'm on my way over to Beard's house."

"Alex, are you nuts?"

"I'm sorry, but I told you I felt like a helpless caged bird. Besides, someone needed to get to Beard's computer. What if someone else thought to retrieve the deleted files?"

"Someone did. Aren't you forgetting the note? What if you are walking straight into a trap?"

"If it's a trap, then it was set for you Jack and not me. That note had your name on it."

"Alex you should know better than I do that it might not matter who walks into that house. Where are you now?" I was already scanning the streets for a cab.

"About a block and a half from the house."

"Walking?" I was stunned she would leave herself out in the open like that.

"Yeah I'm walking. I had no desire to take a cab to Beard's place after what happened last time."

It might actually be one smart move within a much larger mistake. "I'm hailing a taxi and coming for you right now."

"But Jack, what if it's a trap for you?"

"It really doesn't matter at this point."

"Be careful," Alex said sincerely. "I'll be at the house waiting for you." Without another word she hung up.

Chapter 68

The murder of Charles Beard had not garnered any attention from the local authorities or the news. The fact of the matter was there was no murder to investigate. No one reported the initial shooting and Beard's body was still missing. Jack Francis had stumbled across the murder scene but it had quickly disappeared like a figment of his imagination. There was not a single angle to pursue for a murder investigation, and there was yet to be a missing persons report filed. Beard's life spent searching for rare antiques across the world had left him isolated and alone. The neighbors could go months without seeing him and it was no different now. As Alex entered Beard's home, she found the back door unlocked, as Jack had, and everything else almost as Charles Beard had left it.

She was aware that a few people had been through the house before her. Jack, whoever cleaned up the murder, and probably some of Colin's buddies all had a chance to snoop around the place. It was Alex's turn now and she was not about to wait for Jack to show up.

Walking through the house Alex, passed the office where Beard kept his computer and headed up the stairs. Part of her wanted to start working on those deleted files right away, but there was something else she wanted to look for before Jack arrived...something her gut told her she would find. The antique dealer's bedroom was bare, cold, and lacked any resemblance to comfort. Alex thought a more plush accommodation could be found in the old Eastern Bloc. The layout was functional with a bed, a small dresser, and an old, broken desk facing a window to the street below. There were not a lot of hiding places in a room so sparsely decorated, so Alex had high hopes her search would be quick.

The desk became an obvious starting point and she came across a few bills, a checkbook, and a pair of reading glasses. She rubbed the palm of her hand up and down the legs of the desk and underneath it, looking for something small she might have missed. Not wanting to waste any more time, she moved on to the dresser. She felt a little strange going through Beard's drawers, but managed to get through them quickly. When she finished she went over the dresser a second time, looking for any fake bottoms or places she might have missed initially. Coming up empty, she began to worry her hunch was wrong and that she was wasting precious time.

Discouraged, Alex moved on to the bed finding the headboard clean along with the space between the mattress and the box spring. She went as far as lying down on her back and sliding underneath the bed, only coming back out dusty and empty-handed. Alex stood stumped and stunned as she scanned the room one more time. The room was so neat and so lacking that anything out of place would scream out at her, but nothing did. From the silence of the house she heard the sound of a door and she new Jack must have arrived. Alex turned to leave the room and go downstairs to meet Jack, when it suddenly struck her. Quickly and softly she made her way across the room, grabbing the small lamp from on top of the dresser. Smiling to herself as she turned the lamp upside down, she removed a fake lamp base which revealed some wiring and a small memory card. With the excitement of her discovery, she almost missed the sound of voices coming from the first floor.

Chapter 69

"What are you doing here?" I asked as Lee Kershaw pointed a gun at me from behind Charles Beard's desk.

"I should ask you the same thing, Jack. Where is she? I saw her come in."

"I wasn't aware we were on a first name basis, Lee." I made sure to stress the man's name, hoping Alex was somewhere she could hear. Even though I had never actually met Lee Kershaw before I felt like I had come to know him through the investigation. I had to figure he was feeling the same way about me as he sized me up from behind his gun barrel. "Why don't you put that down? We both know you don't know how to use it. Why else would you hire other people to do your dirty work?" I miscalculated the man's capacity to handle a joke, as the beady eyes behind his glasses turned to hate and his mouth curled up in a sneer. If his nerves were as shot as they look, then he might have it in him to shoot me.

"I'll ask you again. Where is she?"

"Who are you talking about?" I knew I was pushing buttons, but I had to stall him long enough to come up with some kind of game plan.

"You know damn well I'm talking about Alex. Now where is she hiding? Alex, come out, come out wherever you are!"

The man's nerves were definitely shot and Kershaw seemed capable of pretty much anything as he moved around the desk and closer to me. "I don't know where she is. If you watched her come in, then you should know I wasn't with her."

"Call her, yell for her to come. Beg your little girlfriend to come save you." Sweat was forming on the man's forehead like rain in a hurricane.

"What's gotten you so worked up, Lee? I always had you pinned as the cool and calm type of criminal."

"You have no idea what you are into Francis. The man is out for blood and there's a good chance we will both end up like Jimmy DeLuca."

It was now even more apparent that Daniel Shaw had gotten his point across with the gruesome way Jimmy was killed. I had witnessed it rattle Alex to the core, but why was Kershaw so unraveled. Didn't he order the hit?

"What is it you want Lee?"

"I want Alex. Now call for her, or you're dead and I'll find her myself."

"Why should I call her if you are going to shoot her too? Besides, how is killing Alex going to help you out? After all, it's your fault she's even in this mess."

"Alex needs to die and it's not by my choosing, but with her out of the picture and Beard's computer properly destroyed, this whole thing will finally be over."

Kershaw had come for the computer as well, that was an interesting tidbit.

"Lee did you get a note sent to you by any chance?"

"That's none of your business."

"I got one too. Don't you see it is a set up? Someone wanted both of us to come here."

"Why would anyone want that?"

There was some hesitation in his voice as he began to rethink the situation. "Someone wants you dead as well," he said with sudden recognition. "I guess I'll have to shoot you too then to find a way back into his good graces. I probably would have done it anyways but now I'll get credit. The credit for finally putting an end to all the problems you've created."

"You're not thinking straight," I said, getting really nervous about my position. "Someone wants you dead as well as me, if that's what the notes were intended for."

"Shut up Jack. I know how to handle this," he said, surprisingly calm as he aimed the gun at me.

I closed my eyes and prayed for the first time in years, as I heard the shot ring out.

Chapter 70

A few seconds passed before I could open my eyes and realized the shot had missed me. When my focus came back, a disturbing scene laid out in front of me. On the floor Lee Kershaw was gurgling his last few breaths of sweet life through a mouth full of blood. He had his gun tightly gripped in his right hand on the floor and aimed out away from his body. I stared down at the man in disbelief remembering my fear only seconds ago of facing this same fate. When I finally saw Alex standing beside me I quickly tried to recover my composure.

"You're welcome," she said smiling at me and giving me a peck on the cheek. It was a kiss of relief for the both of us.

"My savior." I put my arm around her for a moment hoping for a few more seconds to gather myself. "Where did you come from?"

"Upstairs."

"Well, thanks. I owe you one."

"No problem. I wanted to do it anyway after hearing him explain how I needed to be dead." Alex walked over to the dying man and looked down on him with no remorse.

"Any chance he's going to need an ambulance?" I asked, as I walked over to her and kneeled down to get a closer look at Kershaw. He was barely breathing, but his eyes flickered towards me as I got closer. His left hand struggled to move as he went for his pocket. The process seemed to take an eternity, as his breathing grew fainter and the blood dripped from his mouth, down the side of his face. With what seemed to be the last of his strength, Kershaw removed his cell phone and pressed a solitary button before his life left him and the phone dropped to the floor. My first reaction was of fear. Had he just used his phone as a detonator for an explosive device he hid somewhere? As I reached for his cell, I realized my time in the FBI made me think the worst of people.

"What is it?" Alex asked, as she moved closer to me for a better look.

"He must have hit recall. The phone is showing a number but it's not dialing out."

"Call it. He obviously meant for us to talk to whoever is on the other end."

"Or he was trying to send them a warning. I'll hold off on calling the number for now. Maybe Colin can track it down for me later." I put Kershaw's phone into my pocket and stood up walking over to the computer.

"I doubt you'll find anything," Alex said as she moved around behind me to get a view of the screen.

"Why would you think that?"

"If the note was a trap to get you and Kershaw here, then do you really think you will find anything on that computer?"

"Maybe, but it would really take some work to clean out the hard drive."

"Yeah, and it took some work to clean this room up after Beard was shot but someone did."

"I see your point, but I might as well check it while I'm here." I downloaded the retrieval software, then began my search for deleted jpeg files. When nothing came back, I knew Alex was right, but I still began another search for all deleted files hoping to find anything more that could help me. The computer backlog was totally clean and any deeper searching would take someone with expertise way beyond mine.

"It's ok, Jack," Alex said. "We at least have this," and she placed a small memory card down on the desk next to the mouse pad.

"Well, aren't you an impressive one?"

Chapter 71

It was all there. Every photo the Captain had shown me of Chelsea, plus a few close-ups of the body I had never seen before. I wondered if Charles Beard had sent all of these to the Gilmores and the old Captain simply chose not to show them to me. Looking through them again, I couldn't come up with any real angle to play using the pictures. The Zeitlin murder had been officially solved by the local police, and there was no implication of anyone else's involvement or a conspiracy. They certainly could cause the Gilmores some headaches and some unwanted attention. If Charles Beard's body was ever found or he was formally declared missing, then the pictures would definitely show a motive for the Gilmores to want Beard to disappear.

"What are we going to do with them?" Alex asked, still standing behind me as we viewed the files.

"I'm not sure."

"What do you mean? These are the pictures everyone's been hunting for. They're the reason I am in this mess."

Alex sounded distraught at the thought of the pictures being useless. She must have been hoping they would miraculously save her from Daniel Shaw. "Everyone wanted these photos and probably still do, but they don't implicate anyone in the murder, except for Charles Beard's inability to report it, and Chelsea, for being so passed out that she had no idea of what transpired around her. Levi Zeitlin's killer was Jimmy DeLuca, and with him and Kershaw both dead there is only one last connection between these photos and Daniel Shaw."

"Shit." Alex began to pace as she chewed on the tip of her fingernail. "I need to find some kind of leverage to get that man off of my back."

"We do have enough to get him off your back," I realized suddenly.

"What is it?"

"We don't have enough to ever prosecute him, but we probably have enough to keep him away from you." I told her about Levi Zeitlin's phone records and their connection to Mr. and Mrs. Shaw.

"How is that not enough to build a case against him?"

"If we were building a case it would be a good start and a nice theory for a motive, but we're at the end of the evidence line with nothing more to go on. Anything you could testify to would be thrown out as hearsay. It would be a joke to go up against someone as well connected as Daniel Shaw with nothing more than phone records and a story."

"I guess using what we have to get him off my tail is all I can really ask for. I guess I'll go and see him, present what we have, and try to make some kind of deal with the man," Alex said a little more hopeful.

"No. You are going to stay away from Shaw. I'll take Colin and we'll try to meet with Shaw in the morning. If Shaw knows the FBI has made the connections between his wife and Levi Zeitlin, then he will be less likely to lash out on anyone, namely you."

Alex thought it over for a minute as she paced the floor finally stopping at Kershaw's feet. "What are we going to do about him?"

"That will be a tricky one, but let me take care of it."

"Gladly," Alex said as she continued her pacing.

Chapter 72

After emailing copies of the pictures to Colin and myself, I removed the memory card from the computer and pushed it deep into my pocket. Alex was in the front room gazing through the window out onto the quiet street. There was still a lot of work to be done between Kershaw's body lying on the floor and finding a way to keep Alex safe until Colin and I had a chance to meet with Daniel Shaw.

"It's time we got out of here," I said to Alex as I got up from the computer.

"Can we leave?" Alex asked, glancing at Kershaw on the floor of Beard's office from the other room.

"Probably shouldn't, but I need to get you somewhere safe. Don't forget Kershaw got a note too so someone was sending us both here for a reason."

"I was listening and I don't actually remember him admitting to receiving a note."

"Does it really make a difference? You still need to be some place other than here."

"Sorry, I was simply considering other options." Alex was back to looking out into the night. "I wish I could figure out who they sent after Jimmy. It was too outlandish to be the work of anyone I know, or Kershaw's normal lineup of meatheads. Most of Kershaw's minions were like Jimmy, simple-minded hitmen who never thought about the details. Something about Jimmy's murder, the notes, and Beard's missing body makes it all feel different."

"I wouldn't let yourself worry too much about it tonight. Give Colin and me a chance to strong-arm Daniel Shaw a little and it will no longer be your problem." At least I hoped it would be that easy.

"I hope you're right, Jack." Alex finally turned from the window to look at me. "So, what do you do now?"

The words barely left her lips before I heard the window shatter. Alex's eyes went wide as she stared at me with silence and disbelief. Her mouth was open and lost for words. Her hands went to her stomach and blood rushed over them instantly. "Alex!" I yelled out to her, but before I had a chance to move towards her, a second shot found the back of her head. She lingered, frozen in time with her last glimpse of life resting in her eyes, a moment before it was all destroyed, as the bullet passed through and embedded itself into the floor by my feet.

I threw myself to the ground, clawing my way across the floor to her. Her beautiful face was missing and in its place was a mess of tissue and bone. Her right eye twitched and bounced around trying to focus on anything. Alex's mouth was still open, positioned as if to ask God *why*. Even with the fall and the force of the second shot, her hands still clutched her stomach as I rolled her over and pulled her to my lap.

At some point I called Colin, and somehow the house had filled with people, but I have no memory of it. There was a flashback of Colin pulling me from Alex. Another where I was talking to a pair of agents, but none of it registers very well. In my head there is only the sound of a window shattering, and the last, lost expression on Alex's face.

Epilogue

It was six weeks since the night at Charles Beard's house. Since then I pulled myself away from most social activity. Every morning I would leave my condo for a jog along the waterfront, stopping to pick up my daily necessities at the grocer before I returned home. I had no new work to occupy my time, because I had refused to take on any new cases. Colin had been great in tidying up the mess that followed the night at Beard's place, and he only called on my participation when it was mandated by someone above him. Katya was constantly inviting me over for meals and even though I refused more than I accepted, somehow the food still found its way to my door. Colin and Katya made it easier to remember that there were still a few good people in the world.

Early October had brought with it cold winds off of the lake, perch fishing, the changing of the leaves, and Sundays filled with tailgating at the stadium but I was going to miss all of it. My fridge had recently been cleaned out and one simple bag was packed with clothes more suitable to a warmer climate. Someone once sang "I want to go where the weather suits my clothes," and that was what I was doing. The money from the Gilmores could fund my style of living for a time, and even though the money felt dirty I had no intention of returning it. Besides using it to cheer myself up couldn't be all that bad. With the house locked up I tossed the duffel bag over my shoulder and headed off to say goodbye to Colin and Katya.

Walking to the Greenhouse Tavern the sun in the West felt surprisingly warm as it battled the Canadian breeze coming across the lake. When I got to East 4th Street and entered the bar I found Colin had a seat waiting for me. Already in place was a warm plate of gravy frites and a bourbon on the rocks.

"I wasn't planning on staying to eat." I said to Colin as I tossed my bag on the floor and took a seat.

"You've got sometime and besides, when is the next time you'll get to eat fries this good?"

"You may have a point there." I offered Colin a fork and the two of us began to eat in silence. When the plate was clean I sat back in my stool with the bourbon and asked Colin what I had asked him everyday for six weeks. "Any new leads?"

"If I had, you'd be the first to know."

"I don't get it. Maybe I've been out of the game too long, but I could have sworn we had better ways of getting things done when I was still at the Bureau."

"We did, but today our hands are tied down politically, and every move we make has a consequence. When you and I were running around the streets together there was never anyone to answer to as long as we got the job done. Those times are long gone."

"I'm pretty sure everything has gone about as far and as long as it should go."

"What do you mean?"

"Kershaw is dead by Alex's hand and Alex's killer is still out there with no immediate leads to track him down. The two people who started everything, Captain Gilmore and Daniel Shaw, have never been brought up in connection with what happened to anyone from the Zeitlin kid to Alex. The photos of Chelsea have never been leaked, because I can't do it in good conscious and the FBI won't. Better yet Beard's body has never been found so Chelsea can sit comfy in her rehab clinic."

"Don't get yourself worked up." Colin interrupted me. "I never said it was over. You never know we might find something on Alex's shooter."

"What's the point now? Alex is dead because no one knew when to quit. So many people were trying to cover their tracks and get revenge that innocent people had to die. I'm beginning to think its better to have this whole mess over with even if it does end this way. What is there to do anyways? Shaw and the Gilmores are sitting behind a fortress of money and political power, while people like Alex are paying for their actions."

"Look Jack, I'm really sorry about Alex but my hands are tied when it comes to Shaw."

"I know. I wasn't trying to get on your case. I guess I simply need to vent one last time."

"I promise I'll work on finding Alex's killer. In fact it is about all I can do unless someone comes forward with something on Shaw. Who knows maybe his wife will get pissed off enough to talk."

"Let's hope." We sat for a few moments letting the vibe of the conversation cool. "Oh, I almost forgot." I slid my keys across the bar to him.

"House keys?"

"Yeah, the key to the Austin Healy is there too."

"To drive?"

"I need you to get it winterized before the deep freeze sets in, but until then go ahead and drive it. I'll be coming back for it, so no scratches."

"No scratches, I promise."

"Maybe I should have given those keys to Katya." I said as I reached back for them.

"No way. These babies are staying right here. The boys at work are going to love seeing me pull into the garage in your bachelor mobile."

"Great, but keep them out of the driver's seat."

"Promise." Colin made the sign of the cross over his heart. "Did you decide on where you're going yet?"

"Not really. My flight from here will take me to Atlanta but I still need to decide on a final destination from there, probably some small island in the Caribbean or maybe Mexico. I even thought about seeing New Orleans. I haven't been there since the Buckeyes' loss in the National Championship Game."

"Hit me up if you stumble on any fun. I'm long overdue for a vacation."

"I will."

"I spent another half hour talking to Colin and then said goodbye to him and Katya when she came in for her dinner shift. The early darkness of fall was beginning to encroach on the day as I made my way to Prospect Avenue to hail a cab for the airport. When a cab finally pulled up after a few failed attempts I heard a voice behind me as I went to get in.

"Mind if we share this one?" I turned to see a well dressed man behind me. "I'm heading to the airport too, if you don't mind splitting a fare?"

"Sure, why not?" The two of us got in as the cabby threw our bags in the trunk. "Where are you flying to?"

The man turned directly at me for the first time and I noticed how dark the color of his eyes were. "Home to Indianapolis."

"I probably should have guessed that from your strong Midwest accent. It has a touch of Indiana farm boy to it." I said to him half jokingly.

"It still comes through huh?"

"A little. My name's Jack Francis by the way." I extended my hand out to him.

"Reagan O'Neil," he answered with a shake of my hand. "Are you from Cleveland?"

"My whole life."

"So where you headed?"

"Some place warm to escape the winter cold."

"Sounds like a good plan. I'll have to follow your lead someday."

"I'd recommend it." The small talk continued for the duration of the short fifteen minute ride out to the airport. When we arrived the cab driver unloaded our bags and we went our separate ways. The terminal was crowded and I had to wait to check in for my flight. As I waited I fumbled through my duffel looking for my one last connection to the night Alex was shot. Kershaw's phone was towards the bottom of the bag and I stared at it in my hand for a moment, once again reliving the evening. I was awakened from my thoughts by the call to the check-in counter. I slipped the phone into my pocket as I moved from the line. The phone was a connection to that night and a major clue that had never been followed. Kershaw had left a number on it for us to find. The problem was I wasn't sure if I really wanted to know who the number belonged to. I could have given the phone over to Colin and the FBI to trace, but a big part of me wanted this horrible moment of my life behind me.

After convincing the lady behind the counter that my bag was safe for flight, I walked empty handed to the security checkpoint where an agonizing long line confronted me. Above the noise of excited families on their way to Disney and businessmen talking loudly through their earpieces, I heard a ring coming from my pocket. Out of habit I grabbed for the phone and answered it, as I became even more trapped in the slow moving line. "Hello."

"Jack, its Reagan O'Neil."

"What can I do for you?" I began to answer before I realized I was on Kershaw's phone.

"The look on your face is more than enough. It was nice to finally meet you."

The phone went dead and from across the large room designated for airport security, I saw Reagan

O'Neil lift a small bag from the x-ray machine and head down the concourse to his flight.

ABOUT THE AUTHOR

M. P. Murphy was born and raised on the Westside of
Cleveland. He attended Flagler College in Saint
Augustine, Florida, where he also did freelance work for
the Saint Augustine Record. He did his graduate work at
the University of Tiffin, while publishing works on Ernest
Hemingway and Southern history. Currently he resides
with his wife in Charleston, South Carolina.

Look for these and other titles by
MP Murphy at Amazon.com

Titles are also available for the Kindle and for rent
in the Kindle Library